Lies That Bind: Kaedyn's Story

By K. Leigh Michaels

This book is dedicated
to Shan,
because while many sisters are born,
sometimes the best ones just find you;
and to my Mom,
because she is everything a Mom should be
and so much more.
Without them I'd never have made it here.

Acknowledgements

I must first and foremost thank my Heavenly Father. He is my first and true Refuge in times of difficulty and crisis, and He has given me some pretty amazing earthly family – both biological and chosen – to support and love me. He is also the sole Possessor and Distributor of any gifts and talents that may come across as being my own. Without His mercy and grace, my human frailty could never even hope to achieve anything remotely nearing success.

Second only to God is my incredible husband, Randy. Thank you so much for all the love and support that you give me every day, and thank you especially for all the extra love and support you have given me during the long process of writing, editing, re-writing, and publishing this novel. Without you, this could never have been possible.

A huge Thanks goes out to the three oldest of my amazing kids: Ryan, Hunter, and Kaleigh, who, during the writing of this novel, were very patient in sharing their Mom's time with Kallie and Kaedyn, especially in the last days of November 2009, when they would sometimes see me only in the morning before school and at night when I tucked them in. Thank you, my Sweeties. I love you.

These acknowledgements would not be complete without a shout-out to the "National Novel Writing Month" event (nanowrimo.org) and the awesome team that runs it. I've been a writer at heart since I could talk; and though I had written gads of poetry, innumerable short stories, and even a couple of novels by the time I discovered NaNoWriMo, I learned more in that first month than in all the previous years combined.

Kallie

My life was once normal, relatively calm even. Some might even say boring.

I was married to my high school sweetheart, and we had two little girls. The rest of my family consisted of my mom and dad, my sister and brother, and several aunts, uncles, and cousins. I had a teaching job I loved, co-workers that were, for the most part, bearable, and plenty of time to spend with my family and friends.

I inherited red hair, bright green eyes, and a fiery temperament from my mother's Irish family. From my dad, I received an unusual inheritance: the characteristic temper that usually accompanied the hair and eyes had been evened out somewhat by his more phlegmatic personality. The result of the combination was that I was usually pretty patient, but my Irish temper still lurked under the surface, and I could lose my patience rather quickly if pushed over the edge. Thankfully, there was little that pushed me that far.

In short, at the age of twenty-eight, I had it good.

Then my mom got sick, and all the good seemed to both fade into the background and jump into the foreground at the same time.

August 2012

Kaedyn

This can not be happening.

I'm quietly headstrong, and I've even been accused of being idealistic, but I don't really see how that's such a bad thing. I'm certain of my own beliefs, even if I'm not always very vocal about them. One of the things I strongly believe is that no sixteen year old should have to endure watching her mother die.

This can not be happening.

I just kept repeating the phrase over and over in my head. No other words came to mind. This really could not be happening.

I reached up under the long sleeve of my black dress and gripped my forearm, digging my nails into the skin. I had to wake up from this nightmare. Maybe the pain would wake me up, bring me back from this long, never ending, sleepless nightmare.

The preacher droned on just fifteen feet in front of me, but I could not seem to make out exactly what it was he was

7

saying. Something about what a loving wife and mother she was; what a wonderful member of the church she was; what a strong, caring, giving, and just plain amazing person she was.

Was. The word I hated most. The word that stole breath and life from "is" and turned it into the past. My past.

Why did you leave me?

Beside me on the padded bench, my four-year-old niece began to squirm. "Celia," I whispered, "sit still." Celia frowned and crossed her tiny arms over her chest, then continued to kick her dangling legs back and forth. I sighed softly and reached over to pull her onto my lap. Once she was settled into my arms with her head against my shoulder, she fell asleep in about a minute and a half.

The preacher continued to talk, and as everything around me faded slowly into soft lines and pale colors, his voice turned into a quiet buzz in the background.

It seemed only yesterday Mom and I had been having lunch at our favorite little Italian restaurant, talking about college. I had protested somewhat, thinking that two years from now was still such a long way off; but Mom had insisted that I had the best chance at the best colleges and scholarships if I started applying in my Junior year, instead of waiting until my Senior year. We had spread out papers and pamphlets and catalogs from several different colleges, and were having a mixed conversation that included both serious discussion and laughter as I considered the humorous side of going to college. Mom had been regaling me with hilarious stories of her own dorm life. I had not even decided if I wanted to go away to a school where I would likely live in a dorm, or if I wanted to go to a school closer to home and continue living with my parents. Mom was being very supportive in helping me try to decide what I wanted to do, but I could tell she was really hoping that I would at least stay close to home, even if I chose to live in the dorm.

That was near the end of June, only about two weeks before she had gotten much sicker and was no longer able to get out of bed.

Next to me, my sister Kallie reached over and laid her hand on my arm. Startled out of my own thoughts, I turned to look at Kallie, and the blur around me sharpened suddenly. Two-year-old Brooke was lying on the pew, sound asleep with her head on her mother's lap.

"Are you okay?" Kallie whispered.

I nodded, but I could tell by the look on her face that she was not buying it. I shrugged. What was I going to say, "No, I'm not okay"? Kallie gave me that big sister look that basically told me we would be talking about it later and smoothed her hand over Brooke's blonde curls. I rolled my

9

eyes at her and shifted Celia in my arms. For a four year old, she seemed suddenly heavy.

Suddenly, everyone began to slowly stand, and I realized this part was over.

The hard part was over. Next came the harder part, then the hardest part.

Never accuse me of not having a full grasp on grammar, the English language, or superlatives.

My dad, my brother Kurt, my grandpa, and my mom's three brothers all slipped soundlessly from the two family pews and made their way to the front of the auditorium. We had all said our silent goodbyes before the service. Now, each of the men took exactly two seconds to stand in front of the casket and kiss their sister, daughter, mother, wife, on the cheek before moving to their respective positions around the casket. My dad was the last one, and when he had said his final goodbye, he closed the top of the casket. I was sure he had closed it very quietly, but to my ears, the sound of the latch was deafening.

When the men were all in their places, they grasped the handles of the casket and lifted simultaneously with no cue. As they passed each row, the occupants moved from their seats to follow behind; Kallie and her husband Stephen, our grandma, our Aunt Grace, the girls, and I were seated in the first row. Our uncles' families were seated behind us. Beyond that, I

10

didn't know who was in the room. I woke Celia and set her on her feet to walk with us. She clung tightly to my hand. Kallie walked behind us, crying softly; Stephen carried the sleeping Brooke in one arm and held Kallie tightly in the other.

The procession down the center aisle was slow and fast, painful and numb, beautiful and horrific.

And then it was over, and I was riding with Kallie and Stephen, Celia sitting wordlessly on my lap as I stared out the window at nothing. She looked back and forth from my impassive face to her mother's sorrowful one; I could feel the confusion seeping out of her.

The sun was shining, which only pissed me off. It should have been raining; wasn't there a law or something?

Cars stopped at green lights and waited for all of ours to pass. Children and adults alike walking down the sidewalk stopped to stare, silently thanking God or Mother Nature or their lucky stars that it was not them sitting in these cars wishing the world would cave in.

When we all stood in a dense half circle around the rectangular hole cut in the fresh green earth, Brooke and I were the only ones not crying. I was the only one not crying who understood what was happening. Even Celia had tiny tears streaming down her little red cheeks as she watched her beloved Grammy being lowered into the ground. I knew I should have

11

been weeping buckets, but for some reason, neither tears nor emotion would come. I still felt completely numb all over. Celia squeezed my hand, and I looked down to find her gazing up at me through her wide green eyes. Kallie's eyes. Mom's eyes. Bending my knees, I lowered myself into a crouch and pulled her close.

"It will be okay, Ceely," I whispered. She nodded slowly, her eyes dropping to where my hands held hers. I didn't know what else to say to her. I had just made a promise that I wasn't even sure was true. How could I explain to a four year old that her Grammy wasn't coming back?

A loud "smack" startled me, and I turned to see that my father had thrown the first shovel of dirt onto the casket in the hole. Kallie and Stephen led the two little girls to the edge of the grave, where they each tossed in a long-stemmed yellow rose. It was then that I felt the single tear run down my cheek. My dad, uncles, and brother shoveled the rest of the loose dirt into the hole. It was strange to see them dressed up in their pristine black suits and wielding the rough, dirty handles of the shovels.

Finally, mercifully, it was over.

The car drive home was hell. The last thing I ever thought I would do in my life was drive away from my mother forever.

Kallie

The car ride back from the cemetery seemed so long. We all sat in silence in the limo, Stephen's arm around me as I rested my head on his shoulder. Brooke was asleep on my lap, had slept through the entire visitation and service and most of the burial; I was both jealous of her childlike ability to not have to fully comprehend what was happening, and also sorry that the same trait would probably prevent her from remembering her Grammy very well. Celia sat on Kaedyn's lap – while at first glance most people would assume Kade was supporting her niece, I knew the support was actually pretty mutual.

Watching her, it struck me that Kade had only cried once since we'd found out our mother was sick. It had only been six months – which seemed like such a short time when it came to the amount of time we had with her, but such a long time when we had to watch her suffer painfully every day and every night. Stephen and the girls and I had spent nearly every free waking minute at our parents' house, never knowing what moment might be the last; I had even spent the majority of my nights there lately as well.

For the past week, Stephen had been proving that he was the same loving and supportive guy that I had married eight years ago. He would take the girls home at night and put them to bed, so that I could stay with my family and help take care of my mom. Then he would get the girls up in the morning and start getting them ready for school and daycare. I would stay with my family until the clock dragged me away every morning, then rush home to finish getting the girls ready and hustle them out the door, dropping Brooke off at daycare and taking Celia with me to the school where I taught first grade and she attended K-4.

A clinical psychiatrist, Stephen would usually leave the house the minute I got home in order to get to his first appointment, and most nights went from his last appointment straight back to my parents' house, where Kade and I would be making supper while Brooke and Celia spent time with their Grammy and Papa. After dinner, Stephen would take the girls home and start the cycle all over again.

It had been an exhausting routine, but I would have kept it up forever if it would have saved my mother.

Anyway, on those nights, once Stephen and the girls left and I had settled Mom for the night, I would always go into Kaedyn's room and find her lying on the bed, staring blankly at the ceiling. She wouldn't talk to me. She hadn't cried since the day we'd found out Mom was sick, and even then, she had been hiding it. Mom and Dad had been at the hospital, and Kaedyn had come home with us that night. I had found her in the shower in the late hours of the night, sobbing as if her heart was broken in two – and I knew it was. When she got out of the shower, dried off and dressed, she'd let me hold her for a few minutes, but by then the tears had ended, and from that point on it was as if she had vowed not to shed another single tear.

So I would creep into her room at night to find her on top of her completely made bed, in her yoga pants and a long-sleeved tee shirt, staring at the ceiling. I would crawl up onto the bed and lie next to her – just like she used to do when she was a little girl and I was a teenager – and we would just lie there all night, silently. I think one of us would occasionally drift off into a light sleep for a few minutes at a time.

Finally one night – the last night, it turned out to be – Kade spoke into the darkness.

"What are we going to do, Kal? After, I mean."

I didn't know what to say, so I remained silent for several minutes. Finally, I said, "I really don't know, Kade. I wish I did. I guess we just have to. . . take it slowly and make sure we're always there for each other."

15

I could feel the movement of my sister nodding slowly, but I knew she was also rolling her eyes at me. She always rolls her eyes when she thinks I'm being 100% big sister.

Kaedyn

Now that it was over, I didn't know what to do.

We all went back to Mom and Dad's – well, Dad's house. A bunch of people followed our limo in their cars and parked all up and down the street where we lived. Then they quickly filled up our house – the kitchen and the living room and even the back patio – and talked quietly, nibbling off their plates the food that my aunts and grandma had spent the morning preparing.

It all seemed so wrong. Mom had always been the center of any kind of social gathering at our house. To have everyone here without her... the house, though crammed to the corners with people, seemed so empty.

Celia was beginning to sense that things were not right, as well. As we walked up the front walk, she ran ahead to the porch and burst through the front door. "Grammy?" she called. "Grammy, we're home!" I felt my eyes beginning to sting, but I refused to cry; I looked over at Kallie to see that tears were streaming down her face. I stepped forward and took Celia into my arms.

"Grammy isn't here right now, Honey," I said softly.

"But why? I miss her?"

"I miss her too, Ceely," I whispered. "Let's go inside."

And I whisked her off to a corner of the house where no one would dare go today.

We sat silently in the back of Mom's bedroom closet, among her skirts and dresses and shoes, for what felt like a very long time. Finally, Celia spoke.

"Where is Grammy, Kade?"

I took a deep breath. I was not sure how much Celia would be able to understand. But I decided it would be easier to explain more now than to try to explain more later. So I took the plunge. "Well... she's in heaven, Ceely."

Celia frowned. "What she doin' there?"

I felt my eyebrows lift slightly as my empathetic understanding must have passed over my features. I wanted to say that I did not know, that it was not time for her to be there just yet, that she had been in such a hurry to get there that she had forgotten how much all of us still needed her. I wanted to tell Celia that God had made a mistake and taken her instead of someone else whose time it really was, someone who was old and arthritic and on an oxygen tank, who was much better off there than here. I very much wanted to say that I did not care what she was doing there, that no matter what it was, I wanted to be there with her more than anything else.

Obviously, none of these were things I could say to a four year old.

Actually, it probably had nothing to do with her age. I knew I couldn't say any of them to my twenty-eight-year-old sister, either.

What I did finally say made me choke up as I spoke. "Well, Ceely, God had a special job up there, and He needed Grammy to help him with that. And since God knows everything, He knew that He needed her for that job more than we needed her right now. So we had to give her up so that she could help Him with that job."

Celia sat quietly for a full minute, soaking in that information, until I thought she wasn't listening anymore. Finally, she said, "So when God is done with Grammy's job, He send her back home to us, 'cause we need her back again?"

I sighed. "I wish He would, Ceely. But I don't think that's going to happen."

"But why?"

Maybe my brilliant idea of explaining this wasn't so brilliant after all. "Because heaven is forever, Honey. Once you go there, you don't get to come back."

The frown in my niece's forehead deepened as she tried

to grasp "forever." I was pretty sure this was the first time she had ever been presented with the concept. However, the crease in her forehead slowly smoothed away, and her eyes softened as she accepted the explanation. "Okay."

I blinked. "Okay?"

"Okay. I see Grammy when I go to heaven an' see her."

I did not really know what to say to that. She was right – she would see Grammy some day when she got to heaven – but I didn't think a four year old should be thinking about that. Still, I had to admit I had been thinking very similar thoughts lately, and on a much higher level than a four year old's.

Like, how could I get there sooner without actually doing something to hurt myself? I couldn't jump from a building or take pills or slit my wrists.

Because while all I wanted was to be with my mom, there was still – for now at least – a rational part of me that knew I could not hurt my sister and nieces in trying to get to her. So ever since the day we were told Mom had very little time left, I had quit taking the iron pills I was supposed to take every day for my anemia. When I got headaches, I refused to take anything for the pain. And I had quit wearing my seatbelt in the car.

And this is where I'm pretty sure the rest of my life changed.

Kallie

When we got back to Dad's, the sight of so many family members and friends gathered throughout the house caused my own grief to overwhelm me, and my motherly instincts left me for a brief time. So it was at least a half hour before I realized that Kaedyn and Celia had disappeared and that I had no idea how long they had been gone.

Double checking to make sure Stephen had Brooke – I found them at the kitchen table, sharing a plate of crackers and cheese – I went to hunt for my sister and my daughter.

It didn't take me too long to find them. The first place I checked was upstairs in Kaedyn's room, simply because that was her sanctuary. But as soon as I peered into the room to find it empty, I realized that I should have known my sister better than that. She wouldn't have wanted to be in her own space; she would have wanted to be in Mom's space. Sure enough, when I opened Mom and Dad's bedroom door, which was across the hall from Kade's, I found my sister's shoes lying casually on the floor just inside the room. I glanced across the room to see Mom's closet door wide open, and I instantly knew where Kade and Celia were; Dad hadn't been in her closet in a very long time.

I stood for a moment in the doorway, pondering whether to interrupt them or just leave them alone, as long as I knew where they were and that they were safe. It was one of those moments as a mother when I just wanted to do what was best, but I was not quite sure what that was.

I hesitated a fraction of a second too long, and Celia poked her head out from under Mom's favorite dark blue dress. "Hi, Mommy," she said quietly.

The fabric draped around her face brought tears to my eyes yet again, and I quickly blinked them away. "Hi, Baby," I whispered.

Celia crawled out of the closet and ran to me, flinging her arms around my legs. As I held her close, Kaedyn slipped out of the closet. "Sorry, Kal," she said softly. "I hope we didn't worry you."

I shook my head. "Not at all. I just wanted to make sure you were both okay."

"We're okay, Mommy," Celia said from under my arm. "We're just 'membering Grammy."

I looked at Kade, and she gave a tiny, helpless shrug. I looked back down at my daughter. "You and Kade are talking about Grammy?" I asked gently.

"No," she replied, almost indignantly. "We were
'membering Grammy. Just thinking 'bout her, but just doing it
together."

I was amazed that my small daughter could grasp such a
concept. When I looked up at Kaedyn, her eyes reflected the
same surprise.

"Come on, you two. Let's go get something to eat."

Celia turned toward the door, but Kaedyn stood rooted
to the floor. I made deliberate eye contact with my little sister.
She hadn't eaten anything in the three days since Mom had
died, and I could feel myself gearing up for a battle. "Come
on, Kade. You must be starving."

She shook her head slightly, never removing her gaze
from mine.

I paused a moment to make a decision. "Celia, Honey,"
I said, kneeling in front of my daughter, "go out to the kitchen
and find Daddy. He'll get you a plate of snacks."

She looked at her aunt briefly, and then back at me.
"Okay, Mommy." Then she disappeared out the door.

I took a few steps closer to my sister. "Kady," I said in
a near whisper. I hadn't called her that in years. "You need to
eat something. Mom would not want you to do this."

"I'm not hungry, Kallie," she said in a quiet but steel

23

tone. "Besides, I don't want to see any of those people. I just want..." Her voice trailed off. "I just want to be alone," she finished, and I knew that was not what she had intended to say.

I sighed. Maybe she just needed some time. Change had always been hard for her, and this was the worst kind of change. She would eat later, when everyone had gone and she did not feel like her home and her life were being invaded.

"Fine," I resigned. "Can I at least bring you something to drink?"

"Maybe some water."

I nodded. "Okay. I'll be back in a few minutes."

I left the room to check on the girls and get Kaedyn a glass of water. I still wonder to this day if I did the right thing or not.

Kaedyn

It felt like I had won something, even though it also felt like the battle had been instantaneous and weak. But when my sister did not push the issue, I knew I still had some control over a portion of my life, no matter how minuscule.

I didn't really feel like crawling back through everything in my mom's closet, smelling her and feeling her so close when she was really so far away. So I curled up on her side of the bed and hugged her pillow to my chest. It smelled of her shampoo and her lotion and even slightly of her perfume, Eternity. My mind wandered easily off to a time last summer, before she had gotten sick, when she and Kallie and I had taken the girls on a picnic down on the beach.

We had spread one of Mom's handmade quilts on the sand and covered it with sandwiches and chips and pretzels and apples and strawberries and homemade chocolate chip cookies. After we had eaten, the girls had begged to play in the water; so Kallie had rolled up the legs of their shorts and let them wade where the waves lapped up onto the sand. My mom had watched them for just a few minutes before deciding to join them in the fun. Rolling her own pant legs up to her knees, she had run out to the edge of the water and was soon twirling the girls around, dipping their legs in the water and splashing until all three of them were soaked.

Kallie and I had watched them, laughing but declining to join them, neither one of us wanting to get our clothes wet. When Brooke and Celia had grown tired, they all trouped back up to the blanket and lay out in the sun until they were practically as dry as when we had gotten there.

The part I remembered best of that whole day, was watching my mom laughing, with the lake water spraying up around her. That's how I always want to remember her.

Kallie

I found Stephen and the girls and made sure Celia had gotten a snack. They were all sitting on the couch in the living room, watching the home DVD of our family vacation last winter that was playing on the TV. Some other family members, including Dad, and a handful of friends were also gathered in the living room watching the video. There were still quite a few people gathered in the kitchen, eating and talking, and a glance out the back door told me there was also a small crowd still on the back porch. I briefly wondered how long people would stay.

In the kitchen, I grabbed a bottle of water from the fridge, gave one-armed hugs to two of my aunts who were standing there, and ducked back out of the kitchen before anyone else could stop me.

When I got back upstairs, I found Kaedyn asleep on Mom's side of the bed. I figured it was just as well; I knew she hadn't slept much in the last several months. I put the water on Mom's night stand, pulled a quilt over my sister, watched her eyes flutter for a minute or two, and left her alone.

Kaedyn

I spent much of the remainder of August alone; or at least, I felt alone.

One week after Mom's funeral, Dad went back to work. They let him come into the office in the mornings and then work from home in the afternoons. I know he did it so I wouldn't be home alone so much, but I didn't honestly think it made a difference. I was still alone in my room or in the library or the living room or the kitchen. He finally came out of his office at supper time each night, when we would sit together in silence at the table, each alone with our own thoughts, him barely paying attention to whatever meal I had put together that evening, and me playing with the salad I had taken to making for myself every night so that my dad would not get on my case about not eating anything. As long as I had something in front of me, it seemed he did not notice how little I was actually eating.

To be clear, it didn't bother me that my dad was absent in spirit. I just thought it was kind of silly of him to use me as his reason to work from home, when it didn't change anything for me anyway. I think my dad just didn't know how to do anything with his grief other than to block it out with work.

The other change in our house was that two weeks after Mom's funeral, Kurt moved out of his nearby apartment and moved back home with Dad and me. Not much was said about the decision. The night he told Dad he wanted to move back in if it was okay with us, Dad just nodded and patted him on the shoulder.

"Let me know if you want help moving."

"Don't have much stuff. A couple of buddies from work will help me, and we'll have it done in less than a day."

"Okay."

And that was it. I thought it was kind of a weird exchange, but I guess it was just a guy thing. Next thing I knew, Kurt was back in his old room, most of his stuff in a corner of the basement. It didn't make much of a difference to have him living at home, either; he was working about sixty hours a week. I was starting to get jealous of everyone who had these great escapes in their work, where they could just get away any time they wanted to.

I had two weeks of summer left between the time my dad went back to work and the first day of school, and that was part of my problem of feeling so alone. Mom and I had always spent summers together, and the last few weeks before school started were always a mad rush to squeeze in everything we had wanted to do over the summer but had not gotten around to. Trips to the beach, entire days of baking until every counter space in the kitchen was filled up, walking for hours in the woods out behind our house... memories of these things flooded over me one morning as I sat on the back patio with a cup of coffee and a muffin, watching the sun come up.

That was another thing Mom and I had done most mornings in the summer. She had always been an early riser, and she would steal into my room during the wee, dark hours with my favorite hooded fleece sweat shirt fresh out of the dryer, where she warmed it for me. She always had coffee made, and sometimes fresh muffins or biscuits or fresh fruit. And we would sit out on the patio and watch the sun rise.

One summer, when I was twelve, I had wanted to get a dog. I had always wanted a dog, but I couldn't have one, because my dad was allergic. But for some reason, that particular summer I was really wishing I could have had a dog. One week before school, my mom took me to the home of a lady she knew who rescued unwanted puppies to be adopted by other people or families. I spent several hours playing with the puppies and talking to the lady about how she rescued the puppies and then found homes for them. I was fascinated with

31

the whole idea, and had so many questions for her. How did people who were looking for puppies know she had them? How many puppies could she take care of at one time? And my main concern: what happens if no one adopts a puppy that needs a home? She assured me that if no one adopted a puppy, it stayed with her for the rest of its life, which this little twelve year old was very relieved to hear.

And for that one day, I had not one, but fifteen puppies.

The year I was fourteen – and just about to start high school – I had wanted to learn how to cook and bake all kinds of different things, and when we got to the last few weeks before school, I felt like I had not made nearly enough of the things I had wanted to. My mom made an entire week out of that project. We spent a whole day just at a market downtown, picking out all kinds of fresh vegetables and dried fruits, exotic herbs and spices, long braids of papery garlic and huge bricks of cheese: my eyes were full the minute we approached that market, and my mom had just laughed at the way my eyes bulged out of my head. We took everything home and spent four days baking breads and various unusual desserts and handmade candies, ending the week on Friday night with a delicious Italian feast for Dad and Kurt and Kallie and Stephen and the girls: homemade chicken and spinach ravioli al fredo, and my first loaf of Focaccia bread made completely on my own, without a single finger's worth of help from my mom. For dessert, we had tirimisu, which I had been nervous about getting right, and which my mom was so confident would turn out perfectly that it made me even more nervous.

Without Mom here to do any of those things this summer, I spent a lot of my time curled up in the library with a cup of tea and a book. One of Mom's and my favorite rooms had always been the library.

From the time my Mom and Dad were married until Kallie was a toddler, they had lived in a two-bedroom apartment. When Mom got pregnant with Kurt, they had had to look for a new house, with more bedrooms and a yard and maybe even a playroom. Their old place had enough room for a young couple with a toddler, but a second baby meant a growing family.

Mom had told me the story so many times that I could practically hear her voice now as I remembered it. One of her requirements for their next house had been that it have a library. Dad had told her not to get her hopes up, that not very many houses had actual libraries anymore; maybe she could just settle for a couple of nice bookcases in the living room. But my mom stubbornly insisted she needed a real library. They had passed up several houses that, absent a library, were "perfect" houses, according to Dad. They had even passed up

33

a house that Mom had fallen *almost* completely in love with. She just knew their house was out there waiting for them, and it had a library in it.

They had been about to compromise and settle on the other house that Mom had liked almost as much, when their realtor had called them with a house that had just been listed. It just happened to have a library.

Dad was worried that the house would not be as nice as the other one they had been about to settle on, but he agreed to look at it. Lo and behold, the house not only had a library, but it was a beautiful house with four bedrooms, two bathrooms, a finished basement with a family room and playroom, and a huge fenced in yard. It was, in all ways, their dream house.

We had lived there ever since, and my mom had passed her love of libraries on to me. It was also the place where Mom and I had spent the most amount of time together, second only to the kitchen.

So it was only natural that *our* library was my favorite room in the house, especially now. When I curled up in a chair with a cup of tea and closed my eyes, I could feel her there with me.

If I was not in the library reading, or in the kitchen cooking, I was usually in my room. I spent a lot of time listening to music and writing, and the library wasn't private enough for writing; anyone could walk in at any time. Sometimes I would write poetry, but most of the time I wrote in my journal.

My journal had always been my best friend, and here during this time, it still was. I could write things in my journal that I could not tell anyone else. Even Kallie. Sometimes I would read past journal entries and day-dream about telling Kallie what was written in them; the idea always made me shudder. She would never understand the emotions I was feeling or the thoughts I was thinking.

For example, one day when I was feeling particularly lonely and missing my mom, I wrote,

I just don't know how to explain what I'm feeling right now. I feel completely lost without Mom, like I don't know who I am or where I'm going, let alone how to get there. And I feel alone. Not physically alone, but... my soul feels alone. My heart feels alone. I have this pain deep down inside that no one can see and I can't describe, but it hurts so much more than any physical pain I've ever had. It hurts worse than when I fell off my bike and cut my forehead; it hurts worse than when I got pushed off the top of the slide and broke my arm. I don't even feel like the word "pain" is right for what I'm feeling, because it's so much more than any pain I've ever felt. I would

35

rather feel almost any physical pain than whatever feeling this is.

I knew she wouldn't get it, and I was even a little afraid she would be worried. So I kept my thoughts between me and my journal.

One night, a week before school was supposed to start, my dad decided to notice that I had only salad on my plate.

"Aren't you having any of this great lasagna you made?"

"Maybe later, Dad. I'm not really that hungry right now."

He laid down the newspaper he had been reading and frowned at me over the top of his reading glasses. "Not that hungry? What does that mean?"

"It doesn't mean anything except that I'm not hungry right now. Why does it have to mean something other than that?" For some reason, I was suddenly very irritated with my dad. Why had he waited until now to realize I was only eating salad for supper? And why did he even care, anyway?

He sighed. "I just wondered if something was going on, that's all."

I raised my eyebrows at him in a "Dad, you're acting crazy" expression. "Like what?"

"I don't know. Are you worried about starting school?"

"No. I'm looking forward to it, actually." More than you know. Because it means I'll actually have my own place to disappear when I don't feel like dealing with all this.

"Oh, okay. Well... that's good, I guess." There, my old clueless dad was back.

I took a deep breath and exhaled it slowly. I had very nearly just come close to having a fight with my dad, something I had never done in my life.

September 2012

Kaedyn

It hadn't been a lie. I was only too happy to go back to school on the Tuesday after Labor Day.

But no matter how hard I tried or how much I wanted to, I could not concentrate in any of my classes. Chemistry – not the best way to start the morning, by the way – was nothing new to me, so I spent the class hour doodling in my notebook. Next was English Literature, which was usually one of my favorite classes; but since today was the first day, Mr. Brooke had nothing interesting to say other than to go over the list of books and plays and poems we were going to read this year, and to review the various assignments we would be responsible for. I tuned out of United States History the second the bell rang; so I had no idea what they even talked about.

Art was the one redeeming hour of the morning. Instead of talking, Mr. Hudson gave us each a huge sheet of white freezer paper and told us to paint our summer. This was so much better than the "write an essay about the most fun thing you did this summer" assignment that our elementary

41

school teachers had always given us. I happily took my paints and brushes from my bag and set to the task.

I used all my beautiful colors to paint a collage across the entire paper. I painted Kallie and Stephen and Celia and Brooke. I painted Dad and Kurt. I painted myself. And I painted Mom. I painted the ocean waves lapping up on the beach. I painted the woods behind our house, the sun coming up orange and yellow and red over the trees. I painted puppies, and I painted the library. I painted our house, the front porch overflowing with people. I painted a crowd of people standing around a hole in the ground with a casket next to it. I painted Mom's closet. I painted us all together in the upper left hand corner, laughing. Then I painted all of us except Mom in the bottom right hand corner crying.

"Wow," Mr. Hudson said softly as he walked behind me at my table. "Very expressive, Kaedyn. Very alive."

I nodded my thanks and waited for him to pass by me.

Then I opened the lid to my black paint.

And I painted black over the entire paper.

I noticed Mr. Hudson, now standing at the front of the room watching everyone work, raise one eyebrow as he watched what I was doing, but I pretended not to see his reaction.

We left our paintings in Mr. Hudson's room to dry, and he said we could pick them up at the end of the day if we wanted to take them home. That was the other thing I liked about art: Mr. Hudson always let us come back at the end of the day to get our projects, so that we did not have to try to cram them into our lockers or carry them all over the school for the rest of the day. I hadn't decided yet if I even wanted to keep mine.

After art was lunch, which I was absolutely not going to even attempt to participate in. The thought of the crowded and noisy cafeteria was not a happy one, especially today. I decided to hide out in the school library; I doubted that anyone would notice, or at least that anyone who did notice would care.

I couldn't resist a glance into the cafeteria as I passed the closed doors. As I expected, the familiar table on the far side of the room by the windows was crowded with all the same faces that had inhabited it last year. Minus one. Kiera, Emily, Isabel, and Hannah, as well as Kiera's boyfriend Jason and Isabel's boyfriend Luke, were as carefree as ever. They seemed to all be laughing at something Jason has said; not one of their faces held a single trace of evidence that I had ever been part of their little group.

I reflected as I continued down the hall that part of the fault most definitely lay with me. When my mom had gotten

43

sick, I had withdrawn from them, unwilling to give away any of the time I had left with my mom. But I couldn't help but partially blame them as well; not one of them had tried to empathize with me and the pain of watching my mother die by degrees. I knew they couldn't comprehend the loss nor relate to it, but they didn't even try. After a few half-hearted attempts to ask if I was okay or needed anything, they basically shrugged me off and let me go, as if I were no more than a kite they'd grown tired of fighting in the wind.

When I reached the library, I shook my head to clear my thoughts of my ex-friends, and went off to wander. I loved getting lost in the stacks. I loved books so much that I had considered majoring in library science in two years when I went to college.

I finally found something I wanted to read – an old, nearly falling apart copy of Dante's *Inferno* – and took it to a a small table in the corner, sitting in one of the two chairs.

Virgil and Dante were just approaching the Gate of Hell when a shadow fell across my lap and I heard a sharp throat clearing sound. "Ahem."

I looked up. The head librarian, Miss Keenan, was standing there with her arms crossed in front of her chest. I waited expectantly for her to say something.

"Shouldn't you be somewhere right now?"

"Well..." I tried to come up with some clever excuse, but I could not think of one. "It's just lunch." Even to my own ears, it sounded weak.

"Just lunch? Don't you think lunch is important?"

"Not today."

She looked at me skeptically. "And why is that?" she finally asked.

I sighed. "I'm just not... much of a people person."

She frowned. "What about your friends? Don't they notice that you're not eating with them?"

I shook my head. "I really don't have any friends."

Her frown deepened, as if she didn't believe me.

"It's true. I had a really good friend last year, but she moved away over the summer."

It was an outright lie, but it was easier to explain than the truth, and I figured it was an easy enough one to believe. I was right: she nodded sympathetically.

"Well, eating lunch alone isn't any fun at all. I should know; I didn't have very many friends myself as a kid." She looked at me thoughtfully. "Dante's *Inferno*, huh?"

I nodded.

"I haven't seen a high school student read that voluntarily in..." she seemed to be counting in her head, "seventeen years."

45

I had to work hard to keep my face from contorting with surprise. She must have seen something in my eyes anyway.

"Yes, it was me. I was the only one then, too." And then she smiled kindly at me. "Well, if you wanted to sit in here during lunch, that would be okay with me. I doubt any other students are likely to see you, but just the same, let's keep it to ourselves, shall we?"

I nodded in agreement and smiled, and the feeling felt strange to my face. I could not remember the last time I had smiled. "Thank you," I said quietly.

She just nodded and turned to walk back to her desk.

After that, I at least looked forward to the middle of every day. It was my own personal version of heaven on earth, being able to spend an hour in art and then forty-five minutes in the library. School was suddenly much more bearable than I had worried it would be.

It took me only a few days to finish *Inferno*. Then I read John Milton's *Paradise Lost*, which took me a little over a week. On the day I finished it, I had thirty minutes left before the next period, so I went in search of my next read. As I was searching the shelves, Miss Keenan appeared behind me out of nowhere.

"Finished with *Inferno*?"

I turned around, slightly startled. "Yep. And *Paradise Lost*. I was trying to decide whether to read *Inferno* again or start on this," and I held up a copy of *The Iliad* that I had just been flipping through. "I think it might be every bit as boring as I always thought it was, though."

"Well, I have a thought on something that might be more interesting than Homer. Any chance you would want to help me with a project?"

I raised an eyebrow. "You mean, like, re-shelve books?"

She chuckled. "No, I have people for that."

As if on cue, a girl wearing a local college sweatshirt, who did not look much older than I, walked past us pushing a cart of returned books. I watched her for a moment, and then gave Miss Keenan a pointed look. She chuckled again. "This is a specific project you would be helping me with. You would be looking through our electronic lists to find out, first of all, what books we have the most copies of, and secondly, determining if we need all those copies or not. Once you have decided which books we can get rid of some copies of, we'll go through all the copies of those books and take out the most... used... ones."

That did sound interesting. And maybe even a little bit fun. "What would happen to the copies that we take out at the end?"

"Well, you could keep any copies you wanted, as

payment for helping me out. The rest would get donated to a women and children's shelter in the city."

I thought about that for a minute. "Okay," I finally agreed. "I'll do it. But I don't want the books."

"You don't?" Miss Keenan sounded surprised.

"No. I want you to give them all to the shelter."

Miss Keenan smiled. "Okay. Deal."

I spent the last fifteen minutes of my lunch hour learning the electronic filing software that they were running on the library computers. I figured out how to make reports out of the data that was in the system, and by the time I left for study hall, I knew exactly how I was going to start on the project the next day.

I worked every day during my lunch hour for three weeks straight, first pulling a list of the books the library owned by title and quantity, then narrowing the list down to the titles that had more than six copies. Then I analyzed those books by how often they were checked out. A book could be checked out for a maximum of two weeks at a time, so if a book with six copies was only checked out an average of twice a month, the library only needed perhaps three copies. I made a list of the books that were overstocked and how many copies the library could safely remove from the shelves. Once this list was complete, and I had reviewed all the books in the entire library,

Miss Keenan and I physically went through the books and pulled out the most tattered copies.

"I could have one of our college interns do this," Miss Keenan said one day as we sorted through the books. She was seated on the floor, looking at several copies of *The Adventures of Huck Finn* to determine which were the most used.

"No," I said from my perch high up on the ladder, where I was pulling books from the top shelf, near the ceiling. "I like doing this. Besides, I like finishing projects that I started. Then I know it got done right."

Miss Keenan laughed softly in reply.

"What?" I asked, when she did not elaborate.

"You just... sound so much like I did at your age. You're much older than sixteen, you know."

I rolled my eyes. I had always been older than my age. My mom had been telling me that since I was about two years old.

Kallie

My sister was pushing me away. She had not done anything specific; she just wasn't talking to me like she used to. I called her almost every night, but I always ended up doing the talking. The only time she spoke was to give one-word answers to the questions I asked in an attempt to elicit conversation.

On top of my own grief, it was almost too much to deal with. I found I did not have the energy to beg my sister to open up to me, when I began and ended every day missing Mom and trying to figure out how to fight the aching feeling in my heart.

One night on the phone with Kaedyn, I almost yelled at her. I was just trying to get her to talk to me about the general stuff, like school. I understood if she did not want to talk about Mom, but her short answers to my questions about everyday life were starting to frustrate me. In truth, it was really just that I was feeling my own loss very strongly that night, and I was feeling sorry for myself for being too cowardly to bring up the subject that I needed to, simply because I did not want to hurt my sister.

"I miss her, too, you know, Kaedyn!" I had wanted to yell over the phone. "You're not the only one who's hurting!"

But I had gotten a hold of myself. It wasn't Kaedyn's fault. It was less that she was being self-centered and more that she was trying to cope with her own feelings. I had ways of coping that were not available to my sister. I had a family; she had only me.

So that night, I held my girls a little longer when I hugged them before bed. I read them an extra bed time story, and cherished the kisses they planted on my cheek when I tucked them in. When I climbed into my own bed, I snuggled up next to Stephen and let him hold me. When his hands started to roam my body, searching for something that had been difficult for me to give for the last month, I did not hold back. And as we moved together, I discovered that comfort could be found in sometimes unexpected places.

October 2012

Kaedyn

The rest of my classes, aside from art, continued to be a virtual bore. Thankfully, I had never been one of those students who needed the teacher's instruction in order to learn the material. I had always had good self study habits, and tended to remember things after hearing or reading them only once. So for me, doing the homework was sufficient for me to actually learn the material. As long as I kept up with my homework – which I did, because it was the only thing I had to keep my mind from wandering off and dwelling on unpleasant things in the evenings – I continued to ace the tests and earn my straight A's. I had been at the top of my class since first grade, and I did not intend to let that change now.

But during the actual class periods, my mind would wander all over the place. In an effort not to get lost thinking about my mom, I would usually end up drawing in a notebook. Some of these sketches evolved into projects I used for my art class.

In trigonometry, I sat in the corner farthest from the

teacher, so I had a little more liberty with what I could do to occupy my time. Sometimes, I pulled my journal out of my backpack, where I always carried it, and scribbled in it. On the days that were a little bit harder than other days, it helped to write something, even if all I wrote was "Today I miss Mom."

At home, I came out of my room less and less often. I usually forced myself to join my dad and brother for dinner, mostly because I did not want to fight with my dad about it. But once in awhile, when I just felt I could not summon the strength to be there with them, all of us thinking about Mom and feeling her absence together yet separately, I would pull the homework or test card. If I didn't try that too often, my dad couldn't really argue with me about it.

The thing was, I had always thought that it would get better as time went on. That the deep ache in my chest would start to ease up, and I wouldn't always have to force back the tears at every stupid little thing that reminded me of her – because every stupid little thing *did* remind me of her. But it seemed like the longer she was gone, the harder it was to get by without her. I thought it seemed to be that way for Dad and Kurt, too; they both just kept spending as much time as possible at their jobs, and neither of them spoke much when they were at home.

It should also be mentioned that Kallie called me every

single night after Mom's funeral. I knew she was probably worried about me and wanted to know that I was doing okay, but I didn't really know what to say to her. It wasn't like I had anything new and exciting going on either at home or at school. I told her about helping Miss Keenan with the project in the library, but I held back from expressing the enjoyment I was getting from it, and told her about it as if it was just something I was doing to help out, rather than something I really wanted to do.

I don't know why I didn't feel like I could tell my sister how much I really enjoyed helping Miss Keenan with the project; I think I felt a little bit guilty about enjoying something when the loss of my mom was so devastating. And the fact that it was a library project made me feel a little bit like I was betraying my mom, like I should not be working on a project in a library, let alone having so much fun doing it, when she wasn't there to enjoy it, too.

I knew Kallie would tell me that Mom would have wanted me to do something fun, something I enjoyed doing, even something in her honor. But I didn't want to hear Kallie telling me that. I guess that's why I avoided telling her more about it.

It was after one of these phone calls one night in early

October that I crossed the line that I now refer to in my own mind as "the turning point."

Even though I did not feel like I could, I still hated not telling my sister everything. Before, I never would have kept anything from her. Not because I didn't feel I had a choice, but because it was what I had always done. She had always been there, this big sister of whom I was in complete awe. I could not remember not talking to her, even in my preschool years.

Until now, I had kept only one secret from my sister; I was only seven years old when that happened, and not even entirely certain the information I had kept from her could be considered a secret.

So to now intentionally withhold not only information, but also all the feelings that were continually warring inside me, was simply unnatural, and I began to feel guilty about it. After sixteen years of having intentionally kept only one thing from my sister, I now felt like I was no less than outright lying to her every time I talked to her.

During this particular phone call, Kallie, for some reason unknown to me, decided to talk about Mom. She first talked as usual about her day, told me a funny story about a little kid in her class who was learning to tie his shoes and could never quite get the loop through the right hole; she told me about a project that Celia's K4 class was working on for

Thanksgiving, involving decorating their classroom elaborately and making all sorts of various creative foods. She told me that when she had picked Brooke up from daycare, my niece had asked, "When Aunt Kay coming over?" I just lay on my back on my bed, listening to her ramble, and inserting an "uh-huh" in all the right places.

Then she said, "Celia and Brooke have both asked for Grammy today."

I did not know what to say, so I was silent for a moment. When Kallie didn't continue, I said, "Okay."

"Sorry. It was just kind of strange that they both asked, at different times. I guess she's on all of our minds."

Of course she was on all of our minds. Did Kallie expect us all to just forget about her in less than three months? "I guess so."

"Kady?" Kallie's voice had softened. I did not answer, just waited to see what she was going to say. "I have to tell you, I'm missing her a lot right now. You know?"

I nodded, then realized my sister wouldn't see my nod over the phone. "Yeah," I said, my voice strained. "Me too."

And then without warning, I was overwhelmed with feelings of missing her, stronger than they had ever been. I could feel tears starting to well up behind my eyes, but I blinked hard to hold them back. Part of me wanted to cry, but I was too stubborn; I knew that to cry would just make everything worse, cause me to completely fall apart and have no ability to deal with the loss of my mom. I had to stay strong, force my way through the pain of losing her and being without her.

I suddenly wished my sister was here with me, to hold me and tell me everything would be okay. "Kallie?" My voice was near a whisper, but she heard me.

"Yeah, Kade?"

Having to choke back my tears prevented me from speaking for a long minute.

"Are you okay?" my sister finally asked.

"Yeah. I just..." *I miss you. I miss Mom. I need you. I'm in pain. I don't want to do this anymore.* But I couldn't say all of those things. So I just said, "I miss you, Kal."

"Oh, Sweetie. Do you want me to come over there? Do you want to come over here?"

"No, I'll be okay." But even I did not think I sounded convincing.

Apparently neither did Kallie. "How about if I come and get you, and we go for ice cream?"

I thought about that. I really did miss my sister, in spite of the fact that I didn't have a right to, since I was the one responsible for pushing her out. "Okay."

I could almost hear my sister smile. "Okay. I'll be there in fifteen minutes."

"Okay. 'Bye."

"See you in a few minutes."

And she hung up. I listened to the silence for a moment. And I let myself miss the way things were.

My chest suddenly clenched and my heart felt like a tight fist had gotten hold of it. My body and soul were aching for my mom, and I hated myself for pushing my sister out and for not knowing how to let her in. I thought about trying to write in my journal, but there were no words in my head, and I did not have the patience to stare at a blank page and try to search for words that I was starting to believe did not even exist. There just weren't any words to describe the feelings that were washing over me.

I gasped in pain. Looking down, I saw that my hands were clenched into tight fists, and I realized that was where the pain was emanating from. Strangely, it felt much better than the pain that had such a tight hold on my heart.

I forced myself, slowly, to open my hands. There on each of my palms were four short horizontal lines dug deep into the skin, forming a jagged line. The lines from my fingernails were a dark red, but not bleeding. They pulsed with the pain for a few minutes, and when they faded, the pain

ebbed away with them, and the fist in my chest tightened up
again.

But as the internal pain returned, I realized something.
While I had been focused on the pain in my hands, there had
been no other pain. I had been able to breathe. I had just felt...
painless. I needed to find that again. But I needed it to last
longer.

I was sitting with my legs criss-crossed in the middle of
my bedroom floor. My trig book was open in front of me, my
protractor and pencils scattered on the floor just beyond the
text book. I shifted my leg, and found my compass. The tiny
pencil had fallen out.

I don't know where the idea came from, but I knew
what to do with it.

Holding the compass tightly in my fist and using a fair
amount of pressure, I drew it against the thin white skin on the
underside of my forearm. The pain was immediate and exactly
what I was hoping for. Slowly, I made two long and somewhat
deep grooved cuts in the skin, ending about two inches from
the inside crook of my elbow. The lines were an angry red, the
blood glowing through the thin skin as if it was about to spill
over any second, but the cuts did not bleed.

It was so... concrete. I could not explain it any other
way. It pulled me to the center of myself and calmed and

soothed me. And most of all, it took away the pain.

And then I was hooked.

Exactly fifteen minutes later, I was sitting on the front step, wearing my favorite pullover sweatshirt and hugging myself in the cold, when my sister pulled up in front of our house in her black Toyota Camry. Shoving my hands into the pockets of my sweatshirt, I left the porch and went to get in the passenger seat of the car.

Kallie reached across the console to gently rub my arm. I looked up at her. "How are you doing, Sweetie?"

I nodded briefly. "Okay," I said.

We went through the drive-through at a local custard stand, then sat in the parking lot eating our ice cream. This had been a tradition of ours pretty much from the time Kallie got her driver's license. There was something about sitting in the car, next to my sister instead of across from her and feeling confronted, that had always made it easier to talk to her. Having the ice cream gave me something to concentrate on when I did not know how to say what was going through my head at any given time. Tonight was no exception.

"So, what's going on?" My sister spoke after several bites of her chocolate ice cream full of M&M's.

I shrugged, my mouth full of plain vanilla custard. I

swallowed, the cold numbing my throat and making me feel a little better. "Nothing really," I replied.

"How's school?"

"Not any different than last night when you asked me."

Kallie chuckled. "Okay, fair. How are you... feeling?"

"Fine." What else was I supposed to say? *I'm doing terribly, Kallie. I can't live without Mom. I hurt myself tonight because I miss her so much.*

I pressed the inside of my left arm with the heel of my right hand, and the pain helped me hold back the words and the tears.

"How are things going at home? Is Dad around at all, or is he still working all the time?"

"Still working." Kallie's facial expression was one of disapproval. "I don't really blame him, Kal. Besides, I don't mind. It's not like he could do anything..." *To help me.* "... you know, to change anything."

Kallie nodded. "I suppose. What about Kurt? Has he been around at all?"

"Not too much. I think he must be working sixty or seventy hours a week. He's usually home for dinner, though."

Kallie nodded again. I ignored her steady gaze on me as I busied myself with taking another bite of my ice cream. "Maybe we should do this more often," she said thoughtfully.

64

I nodded, pretending to be very interested in my ice cream in order to avoid looking at her.

"I feel like something is wrong, Kady."

My head jerked up. "No, Kallie, why would you think that?" I was suddenly in a panic that she was going to know about the angry red welts on my arm. Rationale left me, and I had the sudden fear that she would somehow just "know" what I had done. And if she knew, she would kill me.

I rested my left arm in my lap, casually laid my right hand over the inside of my elbow, and subtly pressed against the cuts with the heel of my hand. I was calm again, but I kept my arm in my lap, still afraid that if my arm was anywhere near my sister, she would somehow figure out what I had done.

"Nothing in particular. I guess it just... it feels like you're holding something back from me. Is it just that you miss Mom and you don't want to talk about it?"

I took a deep breath. That seemed safe enough to admit to, and then if I did, maybe she would accept that and stop asking questions. I nodded.

"Or is there something else? Something more?"

"It's just... it's just Mom. I just miss her."

My sister's eyes narrowed at me, and her forehead furrowed in an almost-frown. "There's something you're not telling me, Kade."

Why do you always do that? I had to hold back a sigh and a sound in my throat that would have come out sounding like a little growl. My sister's perceptive nature was going to cost me if I was not careful.

"There's nothing, Kallie. I just miss Mom." I tried to sound convincing, but I wondered if I sounded like I was trying too hard.

My sister was not convinced, not even remotely. "I don't believe you, Kade. I know that there is something you aren't telling me, something you're keeping from me. You are the last person in the world who could expect to successfully lie to me." My heart started to pound as the panic rose up in my chest again. "But I'm not going to push it. Just know that you can tell me, whenever you decide you're ready. I'm here." I nodded, grateful that my heart rate was quickly returning to normal. "I'm your sister, Kade. Remember that. I'm your sister, and I love you, and nothing will ever change that."

"I love you, too," I whispered. But the guilt over lying to her nagged at me, telling me that if I really did love her, I would have told her the truth.

Kallie

"I don't know what to do, Kallie." Dad was on the other end of the phone line, and his voice was laced with frustration. "She's going to school every day. She's doing her homework and getting good grades; her teachers even say there is absolutely nothing they can complain about. But she doesn't speak to them; if they ask her a question, she gives one-word answers. Mr. Houghton said that he quit calling on her in Trigonometry, because it takes her too long to complete the problems at the board."

Dad paused to take a breath, and I took the opportunity to interject. "Don't you think she's just trying to adjust to life without Mom? Change has always been harder for her than for the rest of us. She's just trying to work it out in her mind how she's going to get through this."

"Yeah, I know. It just seems worse than that. A couple of her teachers say they don't see her with her friends anymore, and she won't talk to me, either. She comes home from school and goes straight to her room. I've been leaving work early and working from home in the afternoon and evening, so I can be here when she's not at school, but I can't do it forever. There are things at the office that I need to be there to take care of. And I'm worried about leaving her here alone, but I'm also wondering if my being here is even making a difference. I just don't know, Kallie. I don't know if this is normal or not, and I don't know what to do about it either way."

I sighed. The truth was, I didn't know either. I was still calling my sister every night after I put the girls to bed, but she wasn't really talking to me any more than she was talking to anyone else. More often than not, I would ramble about my day, the kids at school, something funny Brooke had done or something cute Celia had said, and when I ran out of things to say, we would sit in silence until I told Kaedyn I needed to go to bed.

But I was starting to form a plan. "Let me think about something, Dad. I might have an idea." What I really intended to do was talk to Stephen about my thought and see what he had to say about it.

"Okay. Just let me know if there's anything you think I should do."

"I'll call you tomorrow night. Love you, Dad."

"Love you, too, Honey. Good night."

"Night."

By the time I had started the dishwasher, used the bathroom, and brushed my teeth, Stephen was already in bed, sitting up with his pillows propped between his back and the headboard, with the blankets pulled up to his armpits and the TV remote in his hand. I quickly changed into my pajamas and crawled in beside him, tugging the blankets up around my shoulders.

"How's your dad doing?" he asked.

"Well, I think *he's* actually doing okay," I replied, "but he's worried about Kade. She's really having a hard time. She won't talk to him. She's not really talking to anyone, actually. Not her teachers, not her friends... I think Dad's worried she won't ever... get over it." I was still having a hard time thinking about Mom's death, too; it had only been a little over two months. I just dealt with it differently than Kade did. "He's concerned about her health, mostly, I think. She doesn't seem to really *care* about anything anymore."

"It sounds like she's probably dealing with some pretty serious depression," Stephen suggested. "Maybe she should see someone. I can suggest someone at the clinic. Or I can find someone at another clinic, if she'd rather."

"Thanks, Babe. That would probably be a good idea at some point, but I'm not sure if she would be willing to talk to a therapist right now."

"Just let me know if you want me to talk to someone," Stephen said, putting his arm around my shoulders. "Or if there's anything else you think I can do to help."

I nestled against his chest. "I was actually thinking about something, and I wanted to see what you thought about it."

"Okay."

"Dad needs to spend more time at the office, but he's worried about leaving her home alone in the afternoons and evenings."

Stephen nodded. "If she has clinical depression, that is a valid concern."

I took a deep breath. "How would you feel about having Kade come and stay with us for awhile? She could stay in the spare bedroom, and her school is right by Brooke's daycare, so I could drop her off and pick her up. Then Dad would know she wasn't alone, and he wouldn't worry about her so much."

"And you would be able to keep an eye on her."

"Well, yes. So Dad wouldn't worry."

"And so *you* wouldn't worry." Stephen's voice was slightly amused.

"Okay, fine, yes, I will worry about her if she's home

alone every night, too."

"That's okay, you know, Kal. She is your sister, after all, and if she's not dealing with... the situation... very well, then you *should* be concerned about her being alone."

"So... you would be okay with it, then?"

"Of course. She would probably help you out with the girls, and it would be good for everyone. Maybe once she settled in, she would start talking to you more about how she's feeling."

"Thanks, Babe." I hugged him tightly. "I really appreciate you understanding."

"That's kind of my job," he chuckled.

"That doesn't mean I don't appreciate it. I love you so much."

"I love you too. Now can we try to get some sleep?"

"Sleep. Right."

Kaedyn

I had managed to slip into the house and get past my dad's study door without him noticing me. Of course, that might have had something to do with the fact that he was on the phone, but I figured that since his back was to the door, there was a good chance he hadn't heard me come in.

When he knocked on my bedroom door five minutes later, I knew I had hoped for too much.

"Come in," I called reluctantly. I had managed to quickly get my Trig book out of my backpack so that I could plead mountainous amounts of homework in the hopes that he would leave me alone shortly.

"You busy, Sweetie?" he asked as he poked his head into my room.

"Kind of," I replied, holding up my open Trig book. It wasn't even open to the right lesson, but he would never know that.

"I'll make it quick. I just want to talk to you for a minute."

"Okay," I sighed. "But I need to get this and my Chem 400 done before bed."

"I'll be quick, I promise."

I nodded, and he pulled out my desk chair to sit in.

"Your sister called me."

What?!?! No wonder he had been facing away from the door when he was on the phone. He had been watching the clock and knew when I would be coming home from school all along.

"I have some things I need to take care of at the office."

I frowned. What did that have to do with my sister? "Okay, Dad. I'm a big girl. I can put myself to bed."

"No, I mean... I'm going to need to start staying at the office longer during the day."

"Oh. Well, that's okay, too. I'm still a big girl, Dad."

"Well, your sister offered to let you stay with her for awhile."

Oh, here we go. The reason my sister called: to stick her nose where it did not belong. "Kallie and Stephen have two little girls and lives of their own. They don't need me getting in their way and interrupting their family."

"Kallie assured me they have discussed it and they both would love to have you there."

"Dad, really, I'm a big girl. I can take care of myself. I don't need Kallie to babysit me anymore."

My dad folded his hands and regarded me for a moment. "Kaedyn, I think it would be a good idea."

Great. I could tell I was past being able to convince my dad. He had already made up his mind. "Just how long did you and Kallie talk?"

"Long enough."

I tightened my jaw stubbornly. "I don't want to go."

"I'm sorry, Kaedyn," he said, shaking his head, "but this is my decision. At least for right now. I need to know that you're going to be okay, and I need to go back to work full time if I'm going to keep my job. This is the best solution I can come up with right now."

"What do you mean? I'm sixteen! Why don't you think I would be okay at home by myself for a couple of hours after school?"

"It might be more than a couple of hours. I might have to work late some nights; I'm going to have to start going on business trips again. It would be better for you to be with someone than to be alone that much. This will be best for now, Honey."

My eyes filled with tears. I was going to lose this battle. "It's not fair, Dad. I don't want... I don't want to go anywhere else right now. I just want to be here."

"You don't want to be here alone, Kaedyn."

"No, I don't. I want to be here with..." I stopped abruptly. I had almost spoken without thinking. "She's here, Daddy," I whispered, blinking furiously to hold back the tears. "She's not at Kallie's. And I want to be here."

My dad swallowed hard. "I know, Honey, I do. I want her to be here, too. But she isn't here anymore, Kaedyn. And staying by yourself just wishing that she was here with you is not good for you. I want you to go to Kallie's for awhile."

I wanted to argue with my dad. I wanted to tell him that he was wrong, that he did not understand, that he had lost his love and his wife but I had lost my mom and my confidante. But instead I nodded. Not because I agreed with him or accepted that I should go, but because I did not have anything left to say.

Finally, my dad spoke again. "I told my boss I would be back in the office full time tomorrow."

"Then you'd better go so I can pack."

"I'm not kicking you out, Kaedyn. Kallie will bring you home any time you want to come home. I promised her I would come to dinner when I can, and she and Stephen will bring you and the girls over for dinner or weekends sometimes. I just need to know you're safe when I'm not around."

"Yeah. And Kallie still thinks it's her job to take care of me."

"Now, don't you blame her, Kaedyn. I am the one who asked her for help. So if you need to be angry with someone, be angry with me."

I shrugged. I did not know what to say. I was upset with Kallie for meddling, frustrated with my dad for letting her. "I need to pack," I said, motioning toward the door.

"Okay. Let me know if you need anything."

"Too late," I muttered as the door shut behind him.

I didn't want to be angry with my dad, but it was hard. Mom never would have shipped me off to someone else. She would have talked to me. She would have tried to help me herself. She never would have asked someone else to step in and take care of her own daughter.

The weird part was that if I really thought about it, other than not wanting to leave the home where I had spent so much time with my mom, in some ways I would much rather have been at Kallie's house than ours. But calling my sister to help him with me... it made me feel like my dad had betrayed me, or given up on me, or not wanted to put the energy into trying to help me himself. And even if I really did feel more at home at my sister's house, my dad's decision made me feel like I did not really belong anywhere.

77

The next morning, I took a suitcase, a duffel bag, and my pillow and blanket to school with me. Thankfully, Kallie met Dad and me in the parking lot just as we got there, and packed all my stuff away in the trunk of her Camry. Then she gave me a tight hug, and left for Brooke's daycare with a promise to pick me up after school.

I had a no harder or easier time paying attention in any of my classes that day than usual; everything was the same haze it had been for the last several months; only now, instead of thinking about how my mom had left me behind, I was agonizing over the feeling that I was the one leaving her behind.

I hadn't told my dad or Kallie, but every night for the last two months, I had slept with her pillow. Dad had never noticed it missing from their bed. I had also begun collecting things: the almost empty Eternity bottle from her medicine cabinet, her favorite pen from beside the telephone, her watch and wedding ring from her jewelry box, a hair clip she had worn out on dates with Dad, and the hospital Polaroid of her holding me just after I was born.

I knew there were more treasures around the house that I would want to keep, but I felt like my dad was stealing my opportunity to find and save them. What if he found things and got rid of them because he could not stand the sight of them or what they reminded him of? Or worse, what if he found things and threw them away, not realizing their importance? The things I had already saved were safe in a little latched wooden box in my suitcase. On some level, I realized my fears were silly ones; Dad was not going to be hunting around for things. He was going to be avoiding places where he might run into anything that would remind him of those little things about her.

The bell signaling the end of the school day startled me out of my thoughts, and I gathered up my Trigonometry text book, notebook, and pencil, and stuffed them into my already full backpack. I had packed everything I was taking home with me prior to Trig, so that I could leave from that class without having to go back to my locker.

As I stepped out into the bright autumn sunshine, I pushed up the sleeve of my sweater to look at my watch. Kallie's school day ended five minutes before mine, but it usually took her at least fifteen minutes to get Celia and wrap things up in her own classroom. Then it would take her five minutes to drive to Brooke's daycare, which was two buildings down from the high school, but would be her first stop because it was on the way from her school to my school. I had plenty of time to walk over to the daycare, which would save Kallie a trip. Besides, waiting there was preferable to waiting at school.

Kallie

When I pulled into the parking lot of Brooke's daycare
and parked facing the chain link fence surrounding the
extensive playground, a surprising sight met my eyes. My two-
year-old daughter was chasing my sixteen-year-old sister around
the slide.

"Okay, girls!" I called as I walked to the gate entrance to
the playground. "Time to go; Mommy's here!"

Brooke's teacher laughed. I stepped through the gate
and initialed the sign-in sheet next to my daughter's name. I
looked up, ready to call the girls again, when Kaedyn suddenly
stopped in her tracks and spun around to catch the squealing
two year old in her arms. Both of them dissolved in a fit of
giggles, and for a brief instant, I was not completely dwelling
on the fact that there was a huge hole in my heart. My love for
the girls filled me up so that for just a few seconds, I forgot that
anything was missing.

Kaedyn noticed me while she was mid-swing with
Brooke. She whispered something in Brooke's ear and pointed

in my direction. My daughter twisted around in her aunt's arms, and when she spotted me, wiggled to the ground and ran to my side.

"Mommy! Kady came to school wis' me today!"

I smiled at them both. "I see that. Are you having fun?" Brooke nodded vigorously. Kaedyn did not say a word, but nodded as she grabbed her backpack from where it was propped against the fence and followed us from the playground to the car. "Were you bored waiting at school?" I asked as I buckled Brooke into her car seat. Celia sat silently in her own car seat and looked from me to her aunt, who was sitting in the front seat with her backpack on her lap.

"No. I just wanted to save you a trip."

I chuckled. "Well, it wouldn't have been that big of a deal, but I think Brooke was happy that you came over to play with her for a little while."

"Yah!" Brooke said emphatically.

The corner of Kaedyn's mouth turned up in the tiniest hint of a smile.

When we pulled into the driveway, I unbuckled Brooke from her car seat, and Kaedyn unbuckled Celia before opening the trunk of the car and beginning to haul all of her stuff into the house.

"Here, Honey, let me help you." I reached for her suitcase, but she held tightly to it. Her duffel bag was thrown over her shoulder, and her arms were full of her pillow and blanket.

"No, I've got it."

And she hurried into the house and up the stairs with a speed I found amazing considering everything she was carrying. Celia watched her go for a moment before turning to look up at me with a quizzical expression on her face.

"She just needs a little quiet time, Baby. We'll leave her alone for a little while. Why don't you come and help me make dinner."

"Okay, Mommy."

Kaedyn

The knock on the bedroom door startled me out of my reverie. As my vision came back into focus, I realized I was staring at my Trig book without actually working on my homework. Then I realized I hadn't answered the door yet.

"Come in," I called.

Kallie stuck her head into the room. "You doing okay?"

"Just working on my Trig homework."

My sister slipped the rest of the way through the door and latched it behind her. "Did you get enough to eat for supper?"

"Yeah, plenty." I tried to concentrate on the problem I was working on, in an attempt to convince Kallie that I was just busy. I did not want her to think I was trying to hide anything from her. Even if I was.

"Because it didn't seem like you ate very much."

"I'm not very hungry right now, Kal. I had enough; I just got full."

I could feel Kallie watching me. But I didn't care. She

might have her suspicions, but she couldn't prove anything. And I certainly wasn't going to give her any indication that she was right. Let her be the one to stew in some self doubt for awhile, for once.

"Okay..." she said, sounding unsure. I could hear her second guessing herself. Good.

I looked up. "I need to finish my Trig, and then I have to study for a history test."

"Okay. Let me know if you need anything."

"Thanks."

My dreams had become filled with food. That night, I dreamed there was a long table stretched out in front of me, covered with ham and turkey and chicken, mashed potatoes and sweet potatoes and rice, homemade bread of all kinds, pasta drenched in al fredo sauce, corn on the cob dripping with butter, muffins and pancakes and cakes and cookies and pies. I could not believe everything before my starving eyes; I dove for the table and began to eat hungrily from every platter within reach. Finally, though I was overly stuffed and feeling very sick, I reached for the plates of desserts.

I woke suddenly with a start and a gasp. Head pounding and feeling full and sick, I clutched my stomach and rolled onto my side, trying to ease away the massive cramp in my abdomen. But the pain refused to dissipate. Finally, somehow knowing there was only one thing that would make me feel better, I got out of bed and crept out across the hallway and into the bathroom.

I had to stay as quiet as possible, because I knew if my sister heard me, I was toast. I had read stories about how you turned on the water to drown out the noise, but I knew that would not actually drown out much noise for more than about a foot radius outside the bathroom. So instead, I turned on the fan. If for some strange reason Kallie or Stephen happened to hear it, I would just say that my stomach was bothering me.

Since I hadn't eaten much for dinner, I didn't throw up very much. But once my stomach was empty, I felt so much better. The pain in my stomach went away almost immediately, and the pounding in my head ceased. I waited for about two minutes to make sure no one had heard me, then rinsed out my mouth and brushed my teeth and crept silently back to my bed.

But even though I felt better than I had in several months, I was not able to find sleep again; I lay for the next few hours unsuccessfully fighting the sleeplessness. The morning came too quickly, and Kallie was knocking on my door to let me know breakfast was ready and it was time to get ready for school.

I knew it was going to be a long day with my lack of

sleep, but I also felt a lightness that I had never felt before.

"And I'm not about to ruin it by eating breakfast," I muttered under my breath as Kallie walked back down the hall away from my room.

Kallie

I woke in the middle of the night, thinking I had heard something. Worrying that one of the girls was out of bed – or maybe that something was wrong with Kaedyn – I lay still and listened for several minutes. But when I did not hear anything, I rolled over and went back to sleep, keeping one ear open just in case.

When the alarm went off, Stephen and I both reluctantly slid out of bed. I took my shower first while he shaved, and then I woke all three of the girls and went down to the kitchen to make breakfast while Stephen showered. Our routine rarely changed.

Once I had some pancakes ready and set in front of Celia and Brooke, I went upstairs to call Kaedyn again. I was slightly concerned that in the fifteen minutes since I had first called her, she hadn't come out of her room; but I passed it off as her first night in a different bed and figured she probably hadn't slept well.

"Kade! Breakfast is ready!"

"Thanks, Kal. I'll be there in a few minutes."

I shrugged and left her alone, returning to the kitchen to check on the girls. Kaedyn had been struggling ever since Mom had died; I fully expected this latest change to be difficult in the immediate future, even if it was for the best in the long run.

So I had to admit to myself that I was not the least bit surprised when Kaedyn came downstairs just when it was time to leave for school. Having showered the night before, she was dressed and carrying a very full-looking backpack.

"No, thanks," she said when I tried to hand her a paper bag with some lunch in it. "I always buy lunch in the cafeteria."

I shrugged. When I was in high school, buying the cafeteria lunch had been the "uncool" thing, but I supposed things changed every few years. Now it was probably less popular to bring your own lunch, and far be it for me to force my sister to be the unpopular one, especially when things were so tough for her right now, and especially with something as silly as lunch. It wasn't like she was telling me it was cool to do drugs.

I herded the little girls out the door behind her and into the car. Celia buckled herself into her booster seat while I buckled Brooke in, and Kaedyn settled her backpack on the floor between her knees.

We drove the first couple of miles in silence. "Did you get all your homework done?" I finally asked.

"Oh, yeah," my sister answered. "I was up a little later than I planned to be, but I got it all done. No problem."

"That's good." I smiled encouraging at her; she offered a weak smile in return.

"I'll walk from here," Kade said when we pulled into Brooke's daycare parking lot. "Save you an extra trip."

"Are you sure? It's not a big deal; I don't mind a bit."

"It's fine. I could use the exercise and a little fresh air."

"Okay," I replied, tugging Brooke out of her car seat and settling her on my hip. Celia followed me into the building, her eyes on Kade until the door shut behind us.

November 2012

Kallie

I guess I'd had some sort of romantic notion that once Kaedyn moved from Dad's house to ours, she would settle in and I would begin to see a visible change in her. I figured it would do her a world of good to get away from the place where she constantly felt Mom's presence.

But she had been with us a month now, and no matter how hard I looked, I could not detect a single change in her demeanor. And she still wasn't talking to me.

I began to give serious consideration to the idea of trying to convince her to talk to a therapist.

Kaedyn

So far, autumn had brought changing colors, but other
than that, little more than a whole lot of rain. Usually by
Thanksgiving, we had at least one really good snow, but it
seemed fitting that we should only have rain this year.

I was not looking forward to the holidays; any of them.
Thanksgiving and Christmas and even New Year's had always
been major family events. Even if extended family had not
been able to be there with us, the five of us – and then the six,
seven, and eight of us – had never been apart for any of these
holidays. With a gaping hole in the family, I did not have high
hopes that these next two months would see us making family
memories that we would want to remember for years to come.

Just thinking about not having Mom with us for the
holidays had me spending more and more time alone in my
room when I was home. And many times, I also used the time
alone to implement my pain-relieving techniques. My compass
and my journal now shared a pocket in my backpack. I had
used the compass several times at school when things hadn't

been so good.

I was quickly filling up my journal – by mid November I had written my way through more than half of the pages. At this rate, the journal would be filled by Christmas. I started to think about finding a new one. The thought made me sigh. Without Mom, I was forced to spend all of my time and share all of my thoughts with a blank book and a pen. If it was Dad who had died, I would be with Mom right now, telling her how I was feeling. We would be sharing our sadness and our memories of him over a cup of hot tea.

Thanksgiving was approaching in just a few days, and it seemed unrealistic to expect the holiday to be anything more than just another day. Actually, I was kind of hoping it would be that way.

A sharp pain in my arm brought me back to the present. I glanced down to see that I had been pressing the corner of my metal protractor hard against my arm, near the inside of my elbow, where I usually cut. Without realizing what I was doing, I had made two wide, shallow cuts in the skin. My heart started to pound and I began to panic. How had I gotten to the point where I was cutting without even knowing it?

This was bad. I had never intended to not be in control of this.

"Kade?" My sister's voice came through the door from

the hallway.

I was sitting on my bedroom floor, and I quickly glanced around to make sure there was no incriminating evidence that I had done something I shouldn't while I was sitting there lost in my thoughts. There wasn't anything except my compass, and that wasn't incriminating since it was lying next to my Trig book. I tugged my sleeve down and took a couple of deep breaths to try to calm myself down.

"Come in."

Kallie opened the door and stuck her head in. "How are you doing?"

"Fine." It had become my standard answer. It was also a code that my sister would never decipher; according to one of my favorite movies, FINE stood for Freaked-out, Insecure, Neurotic, and Emotional. I found it a disturbingly perfect description of my mental state.

Kallie sighed loudly. Despite not knowing my code language, she was tired of hearing the same old answer. She *did* know that I was only saying it because I did not want to elaborate on the honest answer to her question.

"Can I come in for a minute?"

I shrugged. "Sure," I said, motioning to both the floor and my empty desk chair as her seating options.

Kallie chose the floor; in fact, she chose a space that put

her facing me. "So," she said, clasping her hands in her lap. "I've been thinking about Thanksgiving."

"You too, huh?" I muttered. I didn't intend for her to hear me, but she did.

My sister nodded thoughtfully. "I take it then that you're not looking forward to it any more than I am." It was a statement, and not a question.

"That depends. Are you looking forward to it at all, even the tiniest little bit?"

She regarded me for a moment, mulling over her answer in her head. "No," she finally admitted wryly.

"Me either."

Kallie nodded and let out a soft sigh. "And if it weren't for Dad and Kurt, I would probably say, let's just pretend it's any other Thursday."

I liked that idea. A lot.

"But it wouldn't really be fair to do that to them."

"Or the girls," I realized out loud.

"Well, yes, although they're young enough they probably wouldn't know the difference either way right now. But I don't want to leave Dad and Kurt out there alone, when they will probably want to be with the rest of us."

I nodded.

"So I was thinking, maybe we could invite them over

here this year. You and I could make everything; it wouldn't have to be real elaborate, just whatever we feel like making. We could have kind of a relaxed day and just all hang out together."

"Okay," I said. Not because it was necessarily what I wanted to do, but because I couldn't be selfish and tell her that I really just preferred to spend the day alone in my room.

"You're sure you're okay with that?"

I nodded, not a confident nod, but the nod of someone who didn't really have any other option.

"I know," Kallie said softly. "I know you don't want to be with anyone or do anything that will remotely remind you of our past Thanksgivings." I bit my lip and looked up at her. *You know?* "But we need to think of the others right now. Can we do it for them?"

I looked in my sister's eyes for what seemed like a long time. "Yes. I can do it."

She reached across my literature book and took my hands in hers. "Thank you, Kade."

I nodded. I did not trust myself to speak.

Kallie

I had to admit to being pleased that planning for the holidays had gone smoothly. Dad and Kurt had all but jumped at the chance to spend them somewhere different than where we had always spent them when Mom was with us. On Thanksgiving Day, they came to our house around ten in the morning, and we all had a casual brunch. Then while the guys watched football, Kaedyn helped me with preparing the dinner, throwing herself into the task with what I could only define as a steely determination. She had even woken up at five that morning, in order to learn how to stuff and prepare the turkey. She was silent as we worked, only speaking when she needed to ask me how to do something, which, honestly, was not very often.

Dinner was fairly quiet, but not uncomfortable. Dad and Kurt talked a little about work, and Dad asked me about teaching and the girls about school. As expected, the little girls were full of things to say about school, while Kaedyn said very little, only answering direct questions without offering any elaboration. We kept up a casual conversation for as long as we could, but eventually the talk had nowhere to go except to Mom.

It had been silent for several minutes, and I knew everyone was thinking about Mom. I took a deep breath. "I'm sorry if I'm not supposed to talk about her," I said quietly, "but I know we're all thinking about her anyway." All eyes were immediately on me except two. Dad looked at me tenderly, Stephen reached over to take my hand under the table, the little girls' eyes were wide, Kurt's face was impassive, and Kaedyn stared resolutely at her plate. "All I can think about today is when Mom first taught me how to make a turkey." Dad nodded, still watching me, and Stephen squeezed my hand to encourage me to continue. "I thought it was so gross when she told me I had to stick my hand in the turkey to put in the stuffing." Celia and Brook giggled, and I couldn't help but smile at the beauty of the sound.

"Of course," I added, stealing a look at my sister, "Kade didn't even flinch when I told her she had to put her hand inside." Now Kaedyn lifted her eyes from her plate and locked her gaze with mine. Her look was one of warning, but ever the big sister, I ignored it. "Mom really enjoyed teaching you how to cook, Sweetie. She loved it that you wanted to learn. When she wanted to teach me, I didn't want to learn, and… it's something I'll always regret."

Kaedyn began to squirm uncomfortably, so I stopped talking. But I could see that she was fighting to hold back the tears, and I knew I had finally hit the nerve that she had been protecting so vehemently for the past several months.

"Your mom was proud of you all," Dad said. "You may each have different memories, but they are all very special, and I know you'll hold them close forever. Your mom loved you all so much." His voice got tight, and he nodded slowly, then bent back over his plate.

Kurt, who was sitting between Dad and Kaedyn, reached over and gently put his hand on Kaedyn's shoulder. He had never been overly affectionate, but he had always been a very protective brother, particularly of Kade. "I have a lot of memories of Mom, too. But if you guys don't mind, I don't think I'm ready to talk about them right now."

I half-smiled across the table at my siblings. "Of course we don't mind. I just… wanted to share what was on my mind." Kurt nodded. Stephen squeezed my hand again.

It was quiet again, but by that time, everyone was almost finished eating.

A half hour later, I had the table cleaned off, the dishes stacked beside the sink, and the leftovers put away in the fridge. One thing about Thanksgiving was that I probably wouldn't

105

have to cook again until Christmas.

Stephen had disappeared to his office to do some work, and Kaedyn and Kurt were trying to play a board game with the girls. Celia was doing her best to learn the game, and Brooke was doing her best to steal the pieces to play with. Dad and I sat in the dining room, watching the four of them and chatting casually.

"Do you think Kade is losing weight?" Dad suddenly asked.

I was surprised into hesitation. I had noticed no such thing. I looked back over to where my brother and sister and daughters were playing, looking more closely at my sister. She was wearing jeans and an old sweatshirt from my college alma mater. I frowned. She looked the same to me. "No, Dad, I don't think so."

He shrugged. "Okay. I wasn't sure. I just wondered what you thought."

"She's still having a pretty hard time with losing Mom," I said quietly. "I'm sure that's causing her some stress with trying to concentrate in school and everything. It's got to be tiring her out."

"Her report card came in the mail last week. She's still getting straight A's, so somehow, she's still managing to get all of her homework and studying done. And her teachers had nothing but positive things to say in the remarks section."

I nodded. "She's never lacked determination, that's for sure."

"You don't think she's... getting help... from anyone. Do you?"

"You mean cheating?" I was unable to avoid giving my dad a very shocked look. "Of course not." I found it hard to force back a laugh, and something sounding like a snort came out instead. "I'm sorry, Dad, but the suggestion itself is ridiculous. Kade would never cheat."

"I know; you're right. I'm sorry. I don't know why the thought even crossed my mind. Of course she would never do that."

"The truth is," I said quietly, "I don't think she has a lot of contact with other students. I think she's pretty much cutting herself off from other people."

Dad nodded. "I got that idea before she came to stay with you. I was hoping that was just a phase that would pass."

"I'm sure it will; just not overnight. This is going to take time, for all of us."

A few minutes of silence passed, during which Dad took several sips of his coffee and I watched the kids playing and let my mind drift off and take in the warmth and comfort of being here with my family.

"I was thinking," Dad interrupted the silence between us.

I looked up at him, waiting for him to continue. He seemed to be thinking carefully about how he wanted to phrase his next words.

"Well... I mean... Do you think it might be a good idea for Kade to talk to someone?"

I took a few seconds to think before I responded. The same question had passed through my mind multiple times over the past few months, and more specifically, over the last few weeks. "I've been thinking about that, too," I said slowly. "I guess I'm just... not really sure how to approach the subject. I don't think she's going to be open to the idea."

"Yeah, you're probably right."

I waited a moment, to make my next suggestion sound more like a spur of the moment thought. I watched my dad carefully as I spoke. "What would you think about me having Stephen talk to her?" The truth was, I had been considering this for awhile but had been wrestling with whether it would be the best thing for Kaedyn or not.

Dad turned the idea over in his head. "Did you ask Stephen what he thinks?"

"Not yet," I admitted. "I've honestly just been trying to decide whether I should or not."

"I think it's a really good idea."

"You do?"

"Yes, I do. It's kind of a no-lose decision. Even if she ultimately doesn't want to talk to someone else, she's not going to feel threatened by Stephen. And he'll be able to give you an accurate idea of how she's really doing and what she needs."

I nodded slowly. This was the conclusion I continued to come back to, but I had been afraid to make the decision alone. It was good to hear my dad's thoughts reinforcing my own. "Thanks, Dad. I'll talk to Stephen about it."

"Good." Dad took a deep breath and exhaled it in a way that made me think he seemed almost relieved. He must have been worrying about her more than I thought since sending her to our house.

I laid a hand on his arm. "She'll be okay, Dad. Don't worry anymore, okay?"

The corners of his mouth turned up wryly. "Don't be ridiculous, Kallie. I *am* going to worry; I worry about both of you, and Kurt and Stephen, and the girls. I know you're all in God's hands, but I'm a parent, and I have a healthy concern for all of my children and grandchildren. And I always will, no matter how happy and healthy and safe you all are at any given time."

"Okay, fair enough," I said, unable to smile slightly.

"Speaking of which, how are you doing?"

"I'm doing okay, Dad. It helps to have Stephen and the girls to focus on. It's harder sometimes than others, but... I'm doing okay. What about you? Do you need anything? Are you feeling okay?"

"I'm doing... better. Being back at the office helps. I've never wanted to... bury myself in my work to avoid the feelings of... loss. But having something to keep me busy and help me focus on a regular routine... it helps. You know."

"Yes, I do."

Dad nodded. "I'm very thankful we all live so close. I don't think it would be bearable if we didn't. If we weren't able to get together just anytime."

"Yes." I squeezed my dad's arm.

He smiled at me, and in his eyes I could see that everything really was going to be okay.

Kaedyn

It was late Sunday afternoon, the last Sunday of November. We had come home from church and had a simple lunch of sandwiches and soup, and Kallie was putting the girls down for their naps. Like most Sundays, it was feeling like a quiet, lazy day – even more so for me because I had finished all of my Thanksgiving weekend homework the day before. I was tired but not sleepy – I detested afternoon naps – and decided to curl up in the library with a book. There was a fire in the fireplace, and I could bet my sister would join me once the girls were settled in their beds.

I passed Stephen's office on my way to the library, stifling a yawn; the previous night had been a late one, with my dad and Kurt staying until almost midnight. They had spent most of the long weekend here at Kallie's house, and one of our traditional family games of Trivial Pursuit had gone long, as usual.

"Kaedyn?"

I paused. Had I been imagining it, or had Stephen just

called my name? Slowly, I took a step backward and peered around the corner and through the doorway into his office. He was sitting at his desk, which faced the door, working on his laptop; but his gaze was on the door, like he had been expecting a response. Okay, so I hadn't been imagining it.

"You rang?" I said with a slight frown.

My brother-in-law leaned back in his chair. "I was just wondering if we could talk for a few minutes."

I felt my frown deepen with suspicion, but I moved into the room out of sheer curiosity. "Talk about what?"

"Just... you know... how you're doing, how you're feeling."

My eyes widened, and I could feel the creases in my forehead flatten as my frown disappeared into understanding. "My sister put you up to this."

"No, she didn't," Stephen said quickly. "She's just worried about you. She asks me all the time what I think – if I think you're okay; but since you and I haven't really sat down and talked, I can't answer the question honestly. I don't know how you're doing. I've told Kallie that, but still, she thinks I should just know. She asks me every day if I think you're okay. She's worried about you, Kade."

I shrugged helplessly. I didn't know what to say.

"I guess... I just wanted to give you the opportunity to

talk to someone, if you thought it might help."

"Getting shrunk will help?"

Stephen laughed his sincere laugh that I had always loved. His laugh could put a Major General at ease. "I'll never understand why people insist on using that term." His face grew suddenly serious. "I don't believe in 'shrinking' people, Kade. In fact, I don't believe in talking unless I'm asked to talk. I believe in listening to what people have to say, because sometimes, all a person needs is someone to listen *without* talking."

I stood and watched him, waiting.

"I just figured... it's probably hard to think about talking to your dad or Kurt or even Kallie, as close as you two are. Because you know they are all dealing with the same loss you are, and you don't want to add to their burdens or their feelings of sadness. And you love them and you know they love you, and you don't want them to worry about you."

I continued to wait silently. So far, Stephen was hitting the nail on the head, but I was not sure I was ready to give him any indication that he was right.

"They worry about you anyway, Kade. That's why, if you need someone to talk to, I'm the perfect person. You know me well enough to trust me. I think you know me well enough to know that I won't judge you. And then I can easily tell Kallie that you are doing all right, and in turn, she won't worry so much about you."

I regarded him for a moment longer before speaking. "I guess I just don't get why everyone is so worried about me. I mean, Kallie and Kurt aren't getting their heads shrunk, and no one is worried about them."

"Actually, your dad is a little bit worried about all of you, just because losing your mother is such a great loss and difficult thing to deal with."

I crossed my arms over my chest.

"But yes, Kallie and your dad are just a little more worried about you, because you seem to be just withdrawing from everyone. Your teachers say you no longer participate in class, and you haven't seen your friends since before your mom died. You spend a great deal of time alone in your room." I took a breath and opened my mouth to interject, but Stephen spoke again before I could. "And no one is faulting you for that – those are your decisions to make, Kaedyn. But you asked why everyone is worried about you, and that's why."

I nodded. "Well I'm fine. You can tell Kallie that I'm fine."

Stephen watched me for a long minute. "I'm sorry, Kaedyn, but I can't tell Kallie that with any assurance right now. And I absolutely will not lie to my wife."

I hesitated. I didn't want my sister to worry about me. And it might be nice to have someone to talk to, as long as I was careful not to say too much. I was confident I could convince Stephen that I was fine, without letting him know about how I was really feeling, and that he would in turn tell Kallie that she had no reason to worry about me. That was all I really wanted: my sister to stop worrying about me.

"And you won't tell Kallie – or anyone else – anything I talk to you about?" I wanted my bases covered just in case I accidentally slipped. Talking was dangerous; just thinking about it, I could feel myself walking a treacherous line.

"Not unless you tell me you plan to hurt yourself or someone else. Everything else is private and protected."

I considered this. Then I took a deep breath and plunged. "Okay," I said before I could change my mind.

Stephen nodded. "Good. I think you will feel better with someone to talk to. We won't... make it formal or anything. I won't make appointments with you or keep official notes. You just stop in and talk anytime you feel like you need to, okay? And maybe I'll ask you once awhile if you need to talk, just in case you have a hard time asking me to talk. Sound okay?"

I nodded. "Can I... are you busy right now?" There was something I had been dying to get off my mind; keeping it to myself had been killing me, for reasons I could not figure out.

"Not at all." Stephen motioned to the leather wingback chair off to the side of his desk.

I hesitated.

"You can shut the door; it's okay," Stephen said, reading my mind.

"Won't that... bother Kallie?"

Stephen shook his head. "She'll be glad we're talking. She doesn't expect you to talk without a little privacy."

I shut the door quietly and moved across the room to sit in the soft black leather chair.

"So, what's up?" Stephen asked, resting one ankle on the other knee and linking his fingers together around the bent knee.

"See, there's this... thing that I do. And I think that maybe... it's weird. But I can't help it. And I don't want to sound like a freak but... it just helps me feel better when I'm missing my mom."

"Okay. Why don't you tell me about it?"

I hesitated. This was kind of weird. "What if you think I'm a freak?"

Stephen grinned. "Kade, I think everyone is a freak in one way or another. We all have little things about us that make us different. That's what so great about people. We all seem so much alike, but the truth is, we're all individuals and we're all different."

I nodded and relaxed just slightly. "Well, I have these things of my mom's that I've found... you know... all at different times... but I've found them all since... since she died."

Stephen nodded encouragingly and continued to watch me, listening.

"Well, I brought them all with me here. I keep them in this little wooden box my mom bought me when I was a little girl. I keep the box... well I keep it put away, in a secret place."

When I paused to gauge him for a reaction, Stephen spoke. "What kinds of things are they?"

Here's the test, I thought. **This is where the "freak" part starts.**

"Her last bottle of perfume, her watch, her wedding and engagement rings, a hair clip that she loved, the pen she always kept by the phone for taking down messages," I recited the list from memory like a mantra.

Stephen's head tilted slightly to the side. "Anything else?"

I nodded but did not speak.

He raised one eyebrow.

I sighed. "The first picture of her holding me. The one

117

the hospital gives you."

Stephen frowned. "What's the big secret with the picture?"

I shrugged and looked down and my hands locked tightly together in my lap. "It's just... personal, I guess. It all is."

"That's true," Stephen said with a nod. "It is." After a short pause, he said, "Is there anything else."

I nodded slowly. "So, I keep them all in this box. And every night... I take everything out... in a certain order. I look at each thing as I take it out, and I remember something about my mom that it reminds me of. For some of them, like the pen, I can think of something different every single time. For the perfume, I can only think of five things, and I just keep remembering those things over and over. But for... for the picture... I only have one memory. And I'm not even... I'm not really sure what it has to do with the picture." I hesitated, staring at my hands, afraid to look at my brother in law. I found I could not say the memory out loud. So I kept going, hoping he would not notice that I had avoided divulging the memory. "Then... after I've taken everything out and thought of something for each thing... I put everything back in, in the reverse order that I took them out."

I lifted my head to look at Stephen. He was listening,

without any distinguishable expression on his face.

"So... I'm a freak, right? I'm a bigger freak than any of the other freaks you've talked to."

Stephen chuckled. "You're not a freak, Kade. This is pretty normal behavior for someone dealing with grief. Actually, it's kind of mild behavior for the amount of grief you're dealing with."

"But see... shouldn't I not be dealing with grief anymore? I mean, it's been three months... since..." I swallowed hard and forced myself to say it out loud. "Since Mom died. It's been... it's been almost a year since we found out... since we found out she was sick. Shouldn't I be... you know... normal... by now?"

This time when I looked into Stephen's eyes, I thought I saw sympathy there. "Three months really is a short time to deal with grief, Kade. To deal with losing someone who was such a huge part of your life." He regarded me for a second. "Can I ask you a question?"

I nodded, curious and skeptical.

"Have you cried since your mom died?"

I looked back down at my hands. For some reason, I didn't want to tell him the truth, and yet this was one thing about which I would not be able to make up a brilliant lie.

Suddenly, I felt immensely guilty about the fact that I

hadn't cried over my mom's death. "I – I just remembered I need to study for a Chemistry quiz." I knew it sounded lame, and I did not for one second believe that Stephen would not see through my lie. But I needed to get out of there.

Stephen nodded knowingly. "Okay. Talk to you later."

I got up and walked quickly to the door. Then I paused and turned back. "Thanks," I said quietly. He nodded, and I left, escaping to my bedroom.

Kallie

When I walked past Stephen's study on my way to the library after putting the girls down for their naps, his door was closed. At first I paused, wondering if something was wrong; Stephen never worked with his door closed. Then a glance in the library told me that Kaedyn was not there, as I had expected her to be. I concluded that Stephen must have somehow gotten my sister to talk to him.

For a brief second, it felt just a little too weird, thinking of my husband and my sister behind the closed office door.

Then I reminded myself that my life was not a soap opera or a Lifetime movie. Shrugging it off, I continued to the library to find a book and curl up in the chair by the fireplace.

About ten minutes later, I heard the office door open. Curious, but not wanting to be nosy, I listened while keeping my eyes on my book. I recognized Kade's footsteps as she slipped from the room, but I did not hear the door latch shut again. I waited to see what my sister would do, and when I heard her going upstairs, I left my book open on the arm of the chair and went into the office.

Stephen was typing something on his computer when I looked around the corner and through the partially open doorway. He looked up and smiled.

"Hi, Sweetie."

"Hey, Babe. Is... everything okay?"

"You mean with Kaedyn?"

I nodded.

"I think so, at least, immediately speaking. We didn't talk much. I just let her know that I was here if she wanted someone to talk to and didn't want to feel like she was burdening you or your dad."

I nodded again. I should have been glad my sister had an outlet now – and I was – but it still felt a little strange.

Stephen lifted his gaze to meet mine directly and regarded me for a half second. "Are you going to be okay with that? Because if you're not, it's all right; I can find her someone at the office to talk with. Our relationship is more important."

I shook my head. "No. No, of course. I mean, it's fine. I'm glad she'll have someone to talk to, if she needs to."

"My ultimate hope is that she'll talk to you. What she really needs is someone to talk to long term, someone who understands what she's going through and how she's feeling. While I can understand her from the place of experiencing loss, you are really the most ideal person for her to confide in, since you are experiencing the exact same loss she is. And since you will both continue to grieve the loss of your mother on some level for the rest of your lives, it would be best for you to be there for each other. So once she starts to become comfortable with talking through these things in general, I plan to start moving her in the direction of talking through them with *you*."

My eyes widened. "Wow. I guess I didn't really think about that."

"Do you agree? Or would you rather I not set you up with that responsibility?"

"No, I... I completely agree. I think we are the best thing for each other, from the standpoint of being able to understand and empathize with each other."

Stephen nodded. "But of course, Honey, you must let me know if at any time you are not comfortable with the idea of me being alone with your sister. Even if you think you're being silly. I would not want you to ever distrust me or worry about anything."

"Thank you. I appreciate that."

He rose and took me in his arms, holding me close before bending down to kiss me. "I love you," he said huskily.

"I love you, too," I whispered.

That night, I woke again, thinking I had heard something. I lay still, listening to the silence of the house and Stephen's breathing beside me, but heard nothing else. I decided to slip out of bed for a glass of water.

In the hallway, on my way to the kitchen, I saw that the bathroom door was closed and a thin ribbon of light was illuminating the bottom of the door. I leaned up close to the closed door. "Kade?" I said softly.

There was a rustle behind the door. "Yeah?" she replied in a hoarse whisper.

"Are you okay?"

"Yeah." I heard the toilet flush and the water run, and then she opened the door.

"Are you sure you're okay? Are you sick?"

"I'm fine, Kal. My stomach felt like it might be a little upset, but I guess it was really just that I drank about four glasses of water since dinner." She grinned, and I could not help but smile back.

"Okay." I hugged her and kissed the top of her head. "Good night, Kady. Sweet dreams."

"'Night."

I continued to the kitchen for my glass of water, but listened back down the hall to assure myself that she had gone back to bed. I breathed again when I heard her bedroom door open and close behind her.

December 2012

Kaedyn

December was passing with a speed which I could scarcely believe. Soon Christmas would be here, followed by January, February, and then March and spring with it. I had less than six months until the end of the school year. I was about to be a senior. The thought both excited and terrified me.

I had somehow managed to maintain my good grades, though I was still unsure of how I had done that. I barely remembered the school year, aside from the two major events: my mom leaving me and my dad shipping me off to my sister's house. But when second quarter grades came out right before Thanksgiving, I was also given the formal notice that said I was still on track to graduate as the class Valedictorian. That thought, as well, both excited and terrified me.

It was the last Friday of the second week of December, and we had a half day of school, as we were about to start winter break. I had reminded Kallie that morning that I would just walk home that day, and that she shouldn't come by school. I had offered to pick Brooke up and take her home with me, but she had told me not to worry about it, that I could probably use some time to myself. I had been babysitting the girls quite a bit the last couple of weeks, as the end of the quarter had been hectic for her as well – but I never minded helping my sister out.

Anyway, this was how I found myself letting myself into the house at noon with the house key I kept in the tiny hidden pocket of my backpack. I kicked off my shoes just inside the door and dropped my backpack and jacket beside it, promising myself that I would come back later to get all of my stuff and put it away in my room. I was always careful to pick up after myself so Kallie would not have to. Then I went to the kitchen to make myself a sandwich.

As I was cutting my dry, plain turkey sandwich into six equal squares, I thought I heard a sound down the hall. Frowning, I left everything on the counter and moved quietly down the hall toward Stephen's study and the library.

Stephen was standing in front of one of the bookshelves in his office, scanning a row of books with one finger. Hearing me, he turned around, looking startled. "Oh, Kaedyn! I didn't realize you were home."

"I had a half day today," I replied. "I walked home. I was just making some lunch."

He smiled. "Well, you'll enjoy the quiet this afternoon,

I'm sure, without any little toddlers running around." He turned back to the bookshelf. "I didn't have any appointments this morning, so I decided to catch up on some research here at home. Sometimes it's easier to concentrate here where it's quiet."

I nodded. "Well, I guess I'm going to go eat my lunch." I jerked my thumb back toward the kitchen.

"Okay."

I turned to go.

"Hey," Stephen said suddenly. "Are you doing okay?"

I turned back. "Yeah, I guess so." The truth was that I was still feeling the way I had right after my mom had died, but I hadn't felt much like talking to anyone lately, even though I had felt somewhat reassured after that first talk with him.

"You sound uncertain," he said kindly. "I don't have an appointment until three, if you wanted to talk a little bit."

I shrugged.

He shrugged in return. "It's okay if you don't want to talk. I just thought it would be nice to be able to tell Kallie we've talked and you're doing all right."

I nodded. It would be nice to have a way to let my sister know that I was okay. She hadn't asked me how I was doing lately, but I had noticed she was still regularly giving me worried looks.

Stephen jumped on my indecisiveness. "Have a seat," he said, motioning to the black leather couch. "I mean, you know, if you want to." He smiled his easy smile again.

I slid onto the couch and leaned against the over-sized arm, with one leg tucked under me. Stephen continued to search for whatever book he had been looking for when I had interrupted him.

"So how is school going?" he asked.

"Okay," I answered. "We got grades back today. I'm still in place to be Valedictorian. You know, as long as I can manage not to do anything to screw it up between now and then."

He chuckled. "Somehow, I don't think that's going to be a problem for you."

"Yeah, probably not."

He let a few moments of silence pass as he continued to search for the elusive book. "So," he finally spoke again, "how have you been doing? You haven't been back to talk. I'm not sure whether that means you don't really need to talk, or you're afraid to talk about whatever you're thinking and feeling."

I sighed. "Maybe a little of both," I admitted. "I really just don't want to *need* to talk to anyone."

Stephen nodded slowly and then turned away from his

bookshelf to face me. "You've heard of the twelve step process for alcoholics?" I nodded. "Well you know, admitting you could use a little help with something is the first step to just about any process; it doesn't just apply to alcoholics."

"I suppose so."

"It's also the hardest part. And unfortunately, no one can really help you with that part."

"Yeah, I know." I wondered why he was lecturing me on this. Maybe Kallie had asked him to be a little more... persuasive in getting me to talk to him.

"Kade," he said softly, and with the quiet tone of his voice, he had my immediate attention. "It's okay to accept help so you don't have to deal with the difficult stuff alone."

I stared down at my hands and picked at my fingernails. I wanted to believe him, but I did not know how. I could feel his eyes on me for several silent minutes, and then I felt his weight sink down next to me on the couch.

He put his hand on the back of my shoulder. "Why don't you tell me what you're thinking right now, what you're feeling." He began to rub his thumb in slow circles on my back.

Alarms went off all through my head. I tried to push them away. This was my brother-in-law, my sister's husband. He was just trying to help.

Still, it was starting to feel weird.

"I think I'm actually going to eat my lunch. I'm starving."

It could have been my imagination, but I thought I felt his fingers tighten just slightly around my shoulder. "Are you sure you don't want to talk?" He laid his other hand on my leg. "I really think you ought to."

I nodded timidly. "I'm really hungry." My stomach growled in agreement.

And then Stephen was on his feet, and I knew whatever I thought had happened, I truly must have imagined.

"Feel free to stick your head in later if you want. Before three, of course," he said with a wink.

I nodded and fled to the kitchen.

I had never been so confused in my life.

Over the next few days, I did little more than think. Actually, ruminate would have been a better word. My mind turned things over and over and over, replaying those few minutes until that part of my memory had basically turned to mush. I couldn't concentrate on anything else. By Monday night, I was not even sure if I had actually been in Stephen's office on Friday. I was second-guessing myself to a level I had never known could exist.

And on top of all of my self-doubt, I could not stop thinking about what it would do to my sister if this turned out not to be my imagination. Kallie would be in more pain than even my overactive imagination could conjure, if by some crazy way Stephen was attracted to me.

I shuddered at the thought and shoved it out of my head.

I had never – *could* never have – thought of Stephen as anything other than a brother. He *was* my brother; that was all I had ever known him as. I had never even known Stephen when he had not been attached to my sister; I had been so little when they had dated and barely even an adolescent – just eight years old – when they had gotten married. The idea that Stephen could have possibly seen me as anything other than a little sister literally made me sick to my stomach.

That was how I *knew* it had to all be my imagination.

But then... on the slim chance that I was not crazy...

Well, there was just no way I could let my sister get hurt.

No, I was wrong. I had to be wrong. Kallie was not going to get hurt, because nothing had happened and nothing was going to happen.

GAH!! I could hear myself screaming inside my own head. I had to be going crazy.

And this was basically the crazy exercise that my brain

engaged in for about three days straight. And this was how I finally came to a conclusion that covered both possibilities.

I was going to take all of Stephen's words and behaviors with a grain of salt from now on. Even if I had any inkling that his words or actions toward me indicated anything inappropriate, I would ignore him. That way, if it was real, I would not be encouraging him, and maybe he would just quit; and if it was my imagination, I would not make a fool out of myself trying to combat something that was not really there.

Furthermore, I would not cause any pain to Kallie either way.

I threw up fourteen times in those three excruciating days.

Kallie

It was not until Sunday night that I realized Kaedyn had barely come out of her room the whole weekend.

What kind of a sister did that make me?

I told myself that she had probably been in desperate need of some alone time; she had been with me and the girls almost non-stop for three months – nearly a year if I counted the time while Mom was sick. I had done her an unintentional favor by leaving her alone all weekend.

I still had a hard time shaking the guilt over not actually noticing that Kade had been hiding out for nearly three whole days. Pushing it away, I headed up to her room to see if she needed anything.

I knocked softly on the door, and listened for any movement inside. I did not want to wake her if she was sleeping. I heard some scuffling around on the other side of the door, and then Kaedyn opened the door.

"Hey," she said.

Was it my imagination, or was she the tiniest bit out of

breath?

"Hey. I just wanted to see if you were okay. You've hardly come out of your room all weekend. Are you okay? Do you need anything?"

"Oh, no, I'm fine. I just needed some time alone, I guess. Sorry if I worried you."

"No, I wasn't worried exactly. Just want to make sure you're okay." She blinked at me and chewed on her lower lip almost absently. "You know I'm here if you need anything, right?"

"Yeah," she said softly, almost in a whisper.

"Okay." I didn't know what else to say. I could tell she was holding something back, but I was at a loss as to how to get it out of her. *Talk to me!* I wanted to beg her. *Tell me what's going on in that head of yours, and let me help!* But if there was one thing I knew about my baby sister, it was that I could never force her to do anything she did not want to. She had always been that way. "Let me know if you need anything," I could not keep myself from throwing out before I turned to leave.

Kaedyn nodded. "Thanks, Kal." She shut the door quietly behind me.

I started to walk back down the hall, but stopped just a few feet away from her door and leaned against the wall for a moment. ***Help me,*** I thought desperately. But of course, she did not answer. She would never answer again.

Over the next three or four weeks, I noticed several times, in some evenings and on the weekends, that Stephen's study door was closed and Kaedyn was nowhere to be found. I took it as a good sign that she must have been talking to Stephen. Relief washed over me as I thought about her finally finding the ability to deal with her grief instead of pushing it away. But I was very anxious for my sister to begin talking to me again, as Stephen had said she eventually would. Up until this past year, there had been no period of time, even a brief one, where Kaedyn had not confided in me about everything. This silence from my sister was wearing on me.

Kaedyn

Christmas was going to be handled basically the same way as Thanksgiving. Dad and Kurt would come to Kallie and Stephen's house on Christmas Eve and again on Christmas Day. Christmas was even harder than Thanksgiving, because we had to pretend to be happy while we watched the girls squeal with delight as they opened each of their presents. Mom would have been laughing and snapping pictures, having the girls pose with each of their gifts so that she would have over a hundred pictures to choose from for sending to family later. I kept remembering last Christmas.

Nothing spectacular had happened, but I remembered waking up before dawn and going down to the kitchen to find Mom pulling a coffee cake out of the oven. It had snowed overnight, and Mom had cleared the fresh snow off the chairs out on the patio. She had cut two pieces of the hot coffee cake and put them on plates, on a tray with two cups of fresh coffee. She'd motioned to two fleece blankets that she had laid out on one of the dining room chairs; we'd draped the blankets around our shoulders and gone out to sit on the patio and watch the sun rise.

On Christmas Eve, I went to bed when Kallie put the girls to bed. I lay in the dark in my bed, writing in my journal by flashlight and listening for Kallie and Stephen to go to bed. When they did, I looked at my clock and then waited twenty minutes before stealing out of bed.

The new shallow cuts I had made with my protractor two weeks ago had started to fade a few days ago. I had used my compass on them again, to keep them open – and it was sharper than the protractor, but I knew after today that I needed some stronger medicine to get me through Christmas. I had been thinking about it all day, but I had not come up with any ideas, until Kallie got Celia and Brooke's Christmas dresses out and hung them in the living room to let the wrinkles fall out over night. She had noticed a string hanging from the hem of Celia's dress, and had grabbed a pair of scissors from a drawer in the kitchen to cut it off.

Scissors. Perfect.

So now I sneaked out of my room and down to the kitchen, moving quietly through the house so that I would not wake anyone. As soon as I got to the kitchen, I got a glass from the cupboard, so that if anyone *did* come downstairs, I could say I was getting a glass of water.

I did not take the pair that my sister had used earlier that evening; I knew better than to do that. Kallie would miss that pair. Instead, I looked through the "utility drawer," as Kallie called it, and found another, smaller pair, that Kallie never used and would never notice was missing.

I tucked the scissors into my sweatshirt pocket, got my glass of water, and returned upstairs to my room.

Seated safely on my bed, I examined the scissors. They were shiny silver; they looked brand new. I ran my fingers over the blades and found that they were very sharp.

Tugging off my left sleeve but keeping the sweatshirt draped over my shoulder, I felt along my forearm for a good place. I decided against cutting over the top of the protractor cuts. Resurrecting old pain would never get me through Christmas. So I moved to the end of the other cuts, a little closer to the middle of my forearm, and made three slow cuts.

I was not prepared for the sharpness of the scissors, and the first cut went deeper than I had intended. I scrambled for my box of Kleenex as the blood trickled out and ran down my arm. I held a wad of Kleenex against the cut for a minute while I thought about maybe just stopping for tonight.

Then I remembered why I had needed the scissors in the first place.

Last week, a few days after the conversation that had

left me feeling so uncomfortable and confused, Stephen had called me into his study one evening after dinner. Kallie had been giving Brooke and Celia a bath upstairs, and I had been unsure of what I should do. Stephen had been persistent, so I felt I had no choice but to follow him into his office and sit on the couch when he motioned to it. He sat in his desk chair across from me, asked how I was feeling, and reminded me that Kallie wanted me to talk to him so that I could deal with my grief and begin to feel better. He had asked me if I would be willing to keep a journal, and I had admitted that I already had one that I wrote in nearly every day. He had nodded and said that if I was willing to let him read it, it would help him know what I needed to talk about.

I had left his office feeling it had been a very normal conversation, and even chiding myself slightly for my overreaction to the last conversation.

Then this afternoon, he had poked his head into the library while Kallie and I were reading during the girls' naptime.

"Do you have a minute?"

I'd glanced sidelong at my sister, but she had barely looked up from her book when he spoke. I shrugged and got up, leaving my book on the chair, and followed him back to his study.

"I just thought with Christmas coming up, you might

want to talk for a few minutes. I'm sure your mom is on your mind even more now with the holidays."

I nodded hesitantly.

"Have you been writing in your journal?"

"Yes."

"Have you thought any more about letting me read it? I know the idea might make you a bit uncomfortable, but it really would give me a better idea of how to help you."

I was silent for a moment, and I let my eyes wander to the carpet, the bookshelves, the globe... anywhere to avoid his gaze. Finally I said, "It's in my room."

"Would you like to go get it?"

I bit my lip. What he was saying made sense, but I wasn't sure I wanted him reading my most private thoughts. Although, I reminded myself, there weren't any entries about hurting myself or throwing up. The entries were basically about school, missing my mom, and just random memories that occasionally came to me and I wrote down just so I would not forget them. "Okay," I finally said.

I was feeling better about talking to him since our last conversation had been so casual and... ordinary. When I returned with my journal, the study door was closed. I slipped tentatively into the room and found him seated on the couch, his dress shirt partly unbuttoned. I stopped short, my hand

145

half-outstretched with my journal. Had I dropped my guard too quickly?

"It's okay," Stephen said reassuringly. "I just thought the couch would be more comfortable than my chair; I've done far too much work for a Christmas Eve day." He reached over with one hand and patted the space next to him on the couch and reached toward me with the other hand. "Come sit down; let me read a little of what you've written."

His voice was calm and almost sympathetic. I told myself to quit being a drama queen, and went to sit on the couch, handing him my journal. He opened the cover and began to read the first entry.

He only read a few entries, but it seemed to take forever. I had a hard time sitting still while I waited, and I began to fidget, twisting my rings and clasping and unclasping my watch. After a minute or two, Stephen reached over and laid his left hand on my wrists to still my restless hands. I glanced up, but he was still reading my journal. I sat perfectly still and stared at his hands. As he read, he began to move his hand slowly up and down my arm from my wrist to my elbow. When he stopped reading, he closed the journal on his lap with his right hand, his left hand still lightly rubbing my arm. He shifted his position so that his whole body was turned toward me, and reached behind me so that his arm was around my shoulders.

Then he reached over with his other hand to touch my knee. I tried unsuccessfully to suppress a shudder.

"Does this make you feel better?" he asked quietly.

I swallowed hard but couldn't speak.

"I thought it might," he said, as if I had answered him. He began to slowly run his fingers from my knee up my thigh.

"Please," I choked out in a whisper. "Please... don't."

"Well, being a doctor of the mind, I know exactly what that means." He didn't stop. "It means you think we shouldn't be doing this, but at the same time you want to beg me to go farther." His hand moved up the side of my hip. "I'll bet what you're worried about is Kallie thinking we're doing something wrong. But don't worry; we haven't done anything wrong. I'm simply trying to comfort you as you work through your grief over the loss of your mom."

I'd wanted to scream. But his mention of Kallie had given me pause, so I'd clamped down on the inside of my lip to keep from crying out.

He'd stood up from the couch then, abruptly. His final words as he'd returned to his desk still rang in my ears.

"Don't worry. I won't tell Kallie that you were uncomfortable with our session today. Better to avoid any misunderstandings."

Sitting in my bedroom remembering it, I knew I would never get through this Christmas without help.

So I made a second, and then a third cut, being more careful this time to control the depth.

I used a lot of Kleenex that night, since I had not thought about the fact that cuts from the scissors would produce blood. The compass and the protractor had never caused cuts that produced blood. But after the panic over the first cut, I realized that the blood added to the soothing effect of the pain. I wasn't sure how or why; I just felt that the usual comforting feeling was magnified when I saw the blood streaming down my arm.

Finally, I cleaned up my arm, taping some Kleenex over the cuts with Band-aids, buried the bloody Kleenex deep in my waste basket under a pile of crumpled papers, and crawled under my covers.

I was asleep within minutes.

January 2013

Kaedyn

I hated holidays. New Year's was a holiday, even if it was smaller than Thanksgiving and Christmas. So... that tells you how I felt about New Year's.

As much as I wasn't looking forward to New Year's Eve, I figured I would at least be safe from Stephen for one night. After all, Dad and Kurt were over, and the girls were allowed to stay up past midnight. I just assumed he couldn't ask me to come into the office without drawing attention to himself and raising some eyebrows.

By sixteen, I should have learned to never assume.

Kallie was in the kitchen doing dishes when Stephen leaned out of his office.

"Kaedyn, can we talk for a minute?"

Kurt and the girls were sitting next to me on the couch. We were all watching a movie; I thought it was pretty rude of Stephen to interrupt. I glanced sideways at Kurt, hoping he would object to me leaving the movie. He met my gaze and frowned, but didn't say anything. I slowly stood up from the couch and moved toward the study.

"Merry Christmas and Happy New Year," Stephen said as I slowly pushed the door shut behind me. "You haven't given me my present yet."

I tried to block it out, but it was nearly impossible. My skin burned everywhere he touched.

Kallie

The last couple of months had passed pretty quickly, if I actually thought about it. In some ways, it seemed like Kaedyn had just moved in with us, but she had been there for several months now. Thanksgiving and Christmas had come and gone, quietly and surprisingly, pretty painlessly. I was glad that Stephen and I had decided to have Dad and Kurt come to our house for both holidays, as well as New Year's. Without a doubt, the change of venue had been good for everyone – being at Mom and Dad's would have been nothing but painful; but both holidays had been quiet, almost boring.

Now it was New Year's Eve, and we had enjoyed a casual evening of snacks, a movie, and some store-bought firecrackers out in the street. Stephen was in his office; the only days he didn't see patients were actual holidays, so while the girls and I enjoyed a two-week break, he still had to spend some time working at home. Kurt, Kaedyn, Celia, and Brooke were sitting on the couch, watching a movie and waiting for midnight. Celia and Brooke were excited to blow their noisemakers and to see the "big" fireworks on the T.V.

I was cleaning up the dishes from the afternoon, and Dad was sitting at the kitchen table keeping me company.

"I think the holidays have gone well... considering," Dad commented.

"I think so too. The new arrangement worked out pretty well."

Dad nodded. "Hope you and Stephen didn't mind having everyone here so much."

"Not at all," I said fervently, and I meant it. "It was the best thing for all of us."

"I guess we've started a new tradition."

I smiled. "I guess so."

After a minute or two of silence, my dad spoke again, changing the subject. "So... how is Kade doing? Has she talked to Stephen at all?"

Something in my chest tightened, but I wasn't sure why. "Yes," I said slowly. "She's talked to him a couple of times since Thanksgiving."

It hadn't been too hard to reign in my emotions on the matter when I only thought about it, but now that my dad had mentioned the subject out loud, it was hard to stop them from rushing over me like a flood. The main emotion I had been feeling lately was confusion, because I didn't *know* how I felt about my sister being behind closed doors with my husband. It wasn't that I didn't trust either of them; it was just that I had always had an overactive gut reaction to everything, and I had never been good at ignoring it. I found that I was telling a little voice in my head to shut up several times a week.

"Kallie?"

I was yanked back to the present. "Sorry. What was that?"

"I just asked if you thought it was helping."

"Oh. Well…" I had to stop and think about it. Actually, the honest answer would have been that I still had not noticed a change in my sister's habits of withdrawing both socially and emotionally. "Yeah, I think maybe it is helping her to be able to talk about things."

Dad nodded. "Good."

I quickly turned back to the sink full of soapy water and dirty dishes before my dad could read the lie on my face.

February 2013

Kaedyn

Every time I went to Stephen's office – and he was always the one to initiate these conversations now – he continued to reassure me that the best way to deal with my grief was to talk about it, and kept reminding me that what my sister wanted was for me to talk to him so that I could feel better. I knew it was true that my sister wanted me to feel better; she had told me as much herself. And he kept bringing her up in an intimidating, almost threatening way; that was the only reason I went back when he suggested it after that second time that'd had me freaked out.

The times in Stephen's office had seemed to grow quickly in frequency over the weeks; one day I glanced at his calendar and realized it was nearing the end of February. I tried to count backwards to the first time Stephen had talked to me in his office, but the time between then and now was becoming one large, long blur. I had lost track of how many times I had been in his study after the fifth time.

I could remember everything that had happened since

then, but not always in order, and not always with clarity.

I could remember that the day after New Year's, he had begun touching me in places other than my arms and legs. I could remember that he had begun reaching up under my shirt. He had been the one to sit on the couch that time, making me stand in front of him, while he did things to me. I closed my eyes tightly now, trying not to remember it.

But every time was very much the same now – he would sit next to me on the couch, read my journal (though I had stopped making new entries in it), ask me how I was feeling and if I was still missing my mom, ask me if I thought I could talk to Kallie about things, and then start to touch me – and I could not remember what had happened yesterday, and what had happened last week, and what had happened a month ago. He was now constantly telling me that my sister would never understand "what we had," and that she would be terribly hurt by it; but I could not remember if the last time he said it was late on a weeknight, or in the middle of a Sunday afternoon.

I could remember that my sister had knocked on the door once last week, and I could remember that a very strange look had passed over Stephen's face and that he had made some quick, jerky movements before opening the door to let Kallie in; but I could not remember what he had been doing or what he and Kallie had said to each other.

160

What I could remember was that Kallie had left the room, glancing at me before closing the door behind her, as if to say that whatever Stephen was doing with me in there was fine with her.

It was two days after that, that I asked him if we could stop "talking."

"Of course. We can stop any time you want to."

The relief that washed over me was indescribable.

"But you need to know something." My heart sank immediately at his words and the tone with which he spoke them. "We've passed the point at which we can stop without some sort of... repercussions. You see, if we stop now, I feel that I'll need to talk to Kallie about the things that have happened. And if you want me to do that, I will. I'm just concerned that it will hurt her, and I think you should take that into consideration when you make your decision."

I could not believe my ears, and yet I was not surprised. I had known – or should have known – it would come to something like this. On some level, I recognized that the words themselves were simply a blanket, a cover-up designed to make me feel that anything that happened as a result of quitting our "sessions" would be my fault; but the covert threat buried in the words was strong enough to scare me out of wanting Kallie to find out what was going on in Stephen's office.

Other than those few specific instances, what I remembered most often and most clearly were the general emotions that seemed to envelop me constantly now, though the majority of them were feelings for which I did not have words. The only feelings I could find names for were confusion, guilt, and fear. I tried to think through things, tried to understand what it was that was going on in Stephen's study, but I always ended up feeling like my brain was twisted up like a pretzel. I often felt guilty and wondered if I had somehow encouraged Stephen to do these things, wondered if I was doing something to indicate to him that I wanted him to continue. But I could not figure out what I could be doing to encourage him, because every time I thought about Stephen touching me, I felt nothing but revulsion.

Then, of course, there was the fear that Kallie would discover the truth, and blame me, which was way worse than any blame I could lay on myself. And if I lost my sister too... well, that would be far worse than anything Stephen could do to me. Anything I was feeling as a result of what was happening in Stephen's office paled in comparison to the feelings of losing my sister, and so I was willing to withstand anything I had to in order to avoid heaping that major catastrophe on top of my already hopeless existence.

The remaining feelings that I could not name I grouped

into what I could describe only as "pain," and the only ways I could find to ease this pain were either to hurt myself or to make myself throw up.

Last night I had decided that throwing up would be the wiser decision for awhile, because it did not leave any marks behind that Stephen could find.

The last thing I wanted to do right now was give up my cutting, but I had been forced into this decision after the incident a few days before, when I'd had about twelve cuts on the inside of my left forearm when Stephen had called me into his office late in the evening, while Kallie was putting Brooke and Celia to bed. He had motioned for me to sit on the couch while he paced slowly back and forth on the braided rug in front of the couch.

"How are you feeling?" he had asked.

"Fine," I had replied warily. I was exhausted, having had a long day of tests and papers due at school, and did not have the emotional energy to deal with this. I wanted to scream at him to leave me alone. To go jump off a cliff and die. To get the hell out of my life and never touch me or my sister again. But by now I knew such words would bring nothing but punishment.

"What would you like to talk about tonight?"

"Nothing," I said before I could stop myself.

"Now, Kaedyn, you know that isn't an option."

I watched him, afraid of what he was going to do. He stopped pacing and regarded me for a moment. Then he took the few steps to close the gap between where he was standing and the couch, and sat beside me, turning to face me with one leg crossed over the other at the knee. He linked his fingers and propped one elbow up on the back of the couch.

"It sounds like you don't recognize right in this moment that you need some help. That's why it's so good that we are having these little talks. I can help you when you aren't able to recognize that you need help or how to ask for it."

I swallowed hard and tried to keep my face impassive as I met his gaze. I hated the look in his eyes. I had come to expect it, and I hated it more every time I saw it there.

"So I guess this means I should help you decide what you need, since you aren't able to express your needs in words right now."

He edged closer and reached for me. Hands around my waist, he pulled me to my feet as he also stood. "I think you're really going to enjoy this." He spoke so matter of factly, as if there was no question that everything was mutual and factual. He reached up under my chin and unzipped the hooded sweatshirt I was wearing, pushing it back off my arms. I heard it fall to the floor with a soft thud. I swallowed again. He moved so slowly; when would this be over? His eyes roamed over the tank top I was wearing under the sweatshirt, and he nodded with satisfaction. "You can keep that on; it looks nice on you."

Then he unbuttoned my jeans and slowly unzipped them. That was when I started to tremble uncontrollably. "Oh, good," he said quietly. "You're as excited as I hoped you would be." He slowly moved his hands around my waist, lightly touching the skin of my stomach and then my sides and lower back and reaching briefly down the back waist band of my jeans. Then he moved me toward the couch and laid me down so I was lying lengthwise on the couch, my head on the arm rest. He positioned himself over me, one knee on either side of my hips. Then he reached up and gripped both of my wrists in one hand, pulling them over my head.

As he started to pull my jeans down with his free hand, his eyes, roaming over me, stopped suddenly, and he removed his hand from my jeans.

"What is this?" He reached up and gingerly fingered the multiple cuts on my forearm, most of them fresh.

I tried to swallow again, but my dry mouth and the position he was holding my arms in made that very difficult.

"What have you done, Kaedyn?"

I did not know how to respond, so I remained silent.

165

His gaze shifted from my arm to my eyes. "I can see you need more help than I originally thought." He said it almost gently, as if he meant it.

All I could think was, *I've needed more help than you thought ever since you got involved.* I wanted so badly to say it out loud, and I had to bite my tongue to keep the words from coming out.

"It's going to be okay, Kaedyn. I can help you. We're going to make this better."

And with a final caress of the cuts on my arm, his hand slid back down to my jeans.

He was excruciatingly slow as he pulled my jeans down. All I could do was shut my eyes tightly and try to forget it even as it happened.

Kallie

I hated to interrupt Stephen and Kaedyn's talk, but I needed to know if Stephen had given Brooke her cold medicine after supper, so that I could give it to her before bed if he hadn't. I knew they wouldn't mind, but I still felt bad interrupting. I knocked softly on the door and Stephen opened it a moment later.

"Did you give – " I stopped short. Kaedyn was sitting on the leather couch on the other side of the room, hugging her knees to her chest. She looked so... vulnerable. I wanted to rush over and take her in my arms and hold her and tell her everything would be okay. I looked from my sister's face to my husband's face; he was waiting expectantly – almost impatiently, it seemed – for me to finish my question.

I shook my head slightly and started again. "Did you give Brooke her cold medicine?"

"No, I didn't. Was I supposed to?"

"I just didn't want to give her a double dose if you had."

"Oh. Okay. Well, no, I didn't," he said again.

I nodded and looked back to my sister.

"Kallie?"

"Is she – is she okay?" I asked softly.

"Yes, she's fine. She's just having difficulty talking through her memories of your mom."

I nodded again. "Please tell her she can talk to me if she needs to."

"Of course. I will."

I didn't want to leave, but I didn't know what else to do. My sister still hadn't been talking to me, so I figured she wouldn't respond if I tried to comfort her now. Wishing with my whole being that I could do something to help, I left, slowly pulling the door shut behind me.

March 2013

Kallie

I was waking up around two a.m. every single night now. I was actually having a hard time remembering the last time I had slept through the night. I had tried once or twice to just roll over and go back to sleep, but I found the only way I could get back to sleep was to first check on my daughters and my sister.

I wondered if I was developing obsessive-compulsive disorder.

The girls were always in their beds, always sound asleep. More often than not when I peeked into Kaedyn's room, I was overcome with the sudden urge to wake her and hold her. Maybe in the middle of the night, with everything dark and silent, she would talk to me. But I always told myself I was acting crazy and it would be cruel to disturb what little escape my sister had from the pain she was feeling.

Kaedyn

I wondered what was going on with Kallie. Every single morning, usually around two or three o'clock, she would open my door and look in, like she was checking on me or something. She had been doing it for months now. The first time I had heard the door opening, I had been terrified that it was Stephen, coming into my bedroom. But then I had smelled Kallie's perfume as she moved closer to the bed. She had bent over me that time and kissed the side of my forehead.

I had almost started crying right then.

Now that March was half over, I began to count the days until the end of my junior year. I would turn seventeen in the summer, and I was hoping my dad would decide I was old enough to take care of myself and bring me back home.

I honestly did not see myself surviving the summer here, let alone another school year. As it was, I had become lost in a sea of hopelessness. I hated myself. I hated Stephen. Most of the time, it was difficult to tell who I hated more.

It was like my brain was stuck on the rewind button, when all I wanted was to find the stop button.

I didn't know how to get away from him. Not without hurting my sister. I had considered running away, but somehow, Stephen had foreseen that idea. In fact, he seemed to have foreseen almost any possible escape I could ever come up with.

I could not remember exactly when he had said it, but his implications had eventually been put into solid words, and I could remember them exactly and completely.

"Don't even think about telling Kallie about what we're doing, and don't think about running away, either. If your sister gets any inkling of this, whether it's by something you say or do, or something you don't say or do, you'll be sorry. Because I'll tell her the truth about the little slut that you are. She'll see her innocent baby sister for what you really are." He kept saying "what we're doing," like it was mutual. I knew it was intentional, some twisted form of psychological control, but that did not change how guilty I felt.

I had swallowed hard, trying to convince myself that my sister would never believe what he had just said about me, no matter how persuasive he was. But I was terrified that I was wrong, and that if it came down to it, she would believe him over me.

174

And then, as if knowing that self-protection might not be enough of a motivator for me, he added, "And I'll make Kallie sorry you brought her into this. I can do things to her that your baby mind can't even imagine right now."

And then he had done something, something painful, something I could not even bear to remember right now, lying here alone in my dark bedroom. And his unspoken message was that anything he could do to her would be ten times worse.

I wanted to jump out of bed and run to the bathroom with my little scissors and cut until I bled all the pain out.

When my sister came in that night, I had to stuff a corner of the sheet into my mouth to keep from crying out and begging her to make it all stop.

Kaedyn

Near the end of art class one morning late in March, Mr. Hudson stopped behind my chair and said quietly, "I'd like you to hang around after class, please."

Startled, I glanced up to make sure I had heard him correctly. He had already moved on and was several students away now, but he must have seen the confusion on my face, because he caught my eye and nodded once. So when the bell rang, I packed my things up slowly and waited for everyone else to leave.

The only words I could think of to describe Mr. Hudson were "free spirit." He was eclectic, but he was also very open, expressive, and somewhat outgoing, without being obnoxious. He had a personality that exuded energy, and he was good at funneling his energy into his students and their work; to that end, he often stood in close proximity to his students when speaking with them. Today, though, he stood leaning back against his desk, which was a good fifteen feet away from my work table.

177

I sat on my stool, my packed backpack sitting on top of my table, and stared him down. He was the one who had asked me to stay; let him start the conversation.

He continued to watch me for what seemed like an eternity. I was burning with curiosity over why he had kept me after, but I waited patiently. The only thing I was missing right now was lunch, and missing was probably too strong of a word. Finally, Mr. Hudson spoke.

"Kaedyn, I'm a little worried about you."

I raised my eyebrows. Was that all?

"Is there... is there anything going on that you want to talk about?" **Nope.** "Or maybe not that you *want* to talk about, but need to talk about?" **Oh. Well...**

I remained silent, but I could no longer look him in the eye, and my gaze fell to his shoes.

He moved quietly away from his desk and walked around the end of the tables toward me. My heart pounded heavily in my throat. What was he going to do? The closer he got to me, the more panic rose in my chest.

Then he reached behind the tall metal cabinet that stood against the wall behind my stool. From behind the cabinet, he pulled out a solid black sheet of poster paper. I frowned.

"You don't recognize this?"

178

For a second, I didn't. And then… "Oh, yeah. It's the assignment you gave us on the first day of school. But… I thought I said to throw it away?"

"You did. But I didn't. I couldn't." He brought it over to my table and laid it down. "Do you remember what's under here?"

I nodded. I remembered it like it was yesterday.

"Okay. What about this one?" He reached behind the cabinet again and pulled out a stack of smaller sheets of paper. "Do you remember this one? Or this one? Or this one?" He laid the down on top of the black sheet, one at a time. The first was a vast, empty desert with a tiny pool of water in the center. The second was a thunderstorm over a village. The third was rain falling on an empty street and forming blood-red puddles.

I didn't remember any one of them.

I glanced up at Mr. Hudson. He was watching me for a reaction.

"I thought – " my voice caught, and I cleared my throat. "I thought this was art. I thought we were supposed to be creative."

"You were supposed to be creative. And these *are* creative. They also worry me."

I shrugged. "Why?"

"This one – " he held up the desert, "was supposed to be a picture of your life in five years. This one – " he held up the thunderstorm, "was supposed to be a picture of your relationship with your family." I swallowed hard but tried to maintain my impassive face. "And this – " he held up the third picture, and his voice grew very quiet, "was supposed to be a picture of your weekend."

"I'm... sorry," I said very softly. I didn't know what else to say.

Mr. Hudson sighed. "You don't have to apologize. It *is* art. And it's *your* art. You should never apologize for your own creativity. But... Kaedyn, this is nothing like your work from last year. Last year you painted flowers and butterflies. When you painted storms, they had rainbows. You used vibrant colors and large brush strokes. This... it's..." he gestured helplessly toward the paintings. "This is more than losing your mom, Kaedyn. I've seen you five hours a week for the last three years, and even I know that. What's going on?"

His words terrified me. He couldn't know. Kallie would get hurt. And he wouldn't believe me anyway. I shook my head quickly. "Nothing. Nothing's going on. I just – I just miss my mom." My words ran together. I was sure I wasn't convincing him. His eyes told me so.

"Kaedyn..." his voice was almost a whisper. "I know

180

I'm right. Whatever is going on obviously has you believing you can't talk to anyone about it. But... you can. If you... if there's anything I can do, if there's ever a time you feel you need someone to talk to... I'm here. I can help, if you'll let me."

I'd heard that before.

"I'm okay. I – I need to go."

He nodded in resignation. "Okay. See you tomorrow."

I nodded, chewing on the inside of my bottom lip, and grabbed my backpack and tried not to break into a run out the door.

I went to the bathroom instead of the library that day. Locking myself in the stall farthest from the door, I dug into the small pocket of my backpack, past my journal, and grabbed the tiny packet that I had been carrying around since Christmas: the small pair of scissors I had used on Christmas Eve.

Leaning against the cold tile wall with my knees locked, I pulled down the neck of my sweater to expose my shoulder. Just below the front of my shoulder and slightly to the side of my collarbone, I pressed one of the blades into the skin. I cut until my hands stopped shaking and I could breathe again.

Kallie

Kaedyn came in from school one afternoon – she had been walking home every day for over a month – and went straight to her room without a word.

I was in the kitchen, getting the girls their afternoon snack. I sighed heavily. She was isolating herself more and more by the day, and I didn't know what to do about it. Every time I asked Stephen how she was doing, he was vague, saying that she was working through it and that it would take some time. I was getting frustrated.

After getting the girls situated at the table with their snack, I grabbed a bottle of water from the fridge and headed up the stairs to my sister's room, where I knocked lightly on the door with one knuckle.

"Come in." She sounded tired, even through the door.

I opened the door and peered in. Kaedyn was sitting on her bed, pulling books out of her book bag. I sat next to her and held out the bottle of water. "Don't you want a little break before you start your homework?"

183

"Thanks." She took the water, took a sip, and continued pulling out her books.

"How was school today?"

"Fine."

"Kady." She looked at me. "What's going on? You never talk to me anymore. I know how much you miss Mom... Don't you think it would help if you and I could talk about it a little bit?" She didn't answer. "Kady... you're pulling farther and farther away from me, when we should be leaning on each other." She just stared at me. I fought the urge to sigh again. "Do you... do you think it's helping to talk to Stephen?" She turned away from me then. "Is that it? You're not talking to me because it's easier to talk to him? It's okay if it is, I just... I'm worried about you. And I miss my little sister."

"I'm sorry, Kallie," she whispered. "I just... I'm just having a hard time. I don't know what to do."

I gently touched her arm. "Well I'm here if you need to talk." She just nodded. I stood up. "Supper will be ready in about an hour."

"Okay."

As I left her room, I realized it: I was officially a stranger in my sister's life.

April 2013

Kallie

Stephen had his first conference of the year coming up. On Wednesday night, the night before he was leaving for four days, we all sat around the dining room table having dinner, and I tried to explain to the girls that their Daddy would be gone for a few days. Celia understood, but Brooke couldn't grasp the concept.

"Daddy's going bye-bye for a few days. He'll sleep somewhere else at night, and then after four sleeps, he'll come back home."

Next to me, Kaedyn was moving her vegetables around in circles on her plate with her fork. I hadn't seen her put a bite in her mouth yet. She was hovering dangerously close to eating-disordered behavior, for the first time since coming here – and I had been watching for it since the day of Mom's funeral when she had refused to eat anything. "Kaedyn," I said softly, "is something wrong with your dinner?"

"No," she muttered. "It's delicious." I frowned, but didn't say anything else.

Kaedyn began to cut her food up into tiny pieces, then continued to push them around her plate. Suddenly, Stephen slammed his fist on the dining room table, causing all of us except Kade to jump, and Brooke to start crying. "Eat your dinner, Kaedyn!" He demanded, as close to yelling as he could be without actually yelling.

His gaze was locked with Kaedyn's, and when I turned to look at her, I saw in her eyes a mixture of anger, willfulness, and... fear. It was buried, but it was definitely there. It terrified me to see my sister looking at my husband with such near-hatred.

"Stephen! Stop it!" His frowned deepened, and I could see he was about to make this a battle of stubbornness. I was appalled that he thought he could talk to my sister like she was his child. "I'm serious. Lay off." Grinding his teeth, he went back to his own plate of food.

I fully expected my sister to beg off dinner and escape to her room, but she didn't. She even ate a few bites of the food on her plate.

After dinner, she helped me clear the table and load the dishwasher. Then she followed me up to the nursery when I put the girls to bed, and back down to the library, where she snuggled up next to me on the couch with a book for two blissful hours. It was almost like I had my old little sister back for awhile. After our short talk in her room that afternoon, it was the strangest thing.

I tried to put the pieces together, but when I couldn't, I shrugged it all off as just a bizarre evening.

Kaedyn

I lay on top of my neatly made bed, not having bothered to pull back the quilt, with my face turned to the moonlight streaming through the window. I was staring out into the night, but I was not focused on anything in particular; the pinpoints of the stars blurred against the night sky, and I took them in all at once, and not at all.

I hadn't slept much that night, which really was not unusual lately, but tonight I wished I didn't even have to go to bed. After spending the evening with Kallie, I had been virtually terrified to be out of her sight. It took every ounce of strength in me not to beg her to stay in my room with me that night.

It was probably about four in the morning now. I had just sneaked back from the bathroom, where I had thrown up for the eighth or ninth time in about six hours. I was sure that every bit of the few bites of mashed potatoes, green beans, and chicken I had had for supper was out of me now. I was exhausted from head to toe and everywhere in between, but I could not remember the last time I had slept for more than twenty or thirty minutes without waking up. I was pretty sure I spent more time in the bathroom these days than I spent sleeping.

I reached down and felt my flat stomach, ran my fingers up to my collar bone. Losing weight had never been my goal, but I had noticed in the last couple of months that I had actually lost quite a bit of weight. I was surprised that my sister hadn't noticed, but I had also been very careful to hide it. I had bought a couple of pairs of smaller jeans, so that Kallie would not notice how loose the others were on me, and I now had an extensive collection of over-sized sweatshirts.

All I really wanted – all I had ever wanted – was to feel better. And for those few seconds that I had my finger in my throat and felt the gagging sensation, for the few minutes that I felt my body getting rid of the contents of my stomach, I did feel better. Better than I had in over a year, except for the cutting. I had been trying hard not to cut lately, ever since Stephen had used it as an excuse to do even more horrible things to me, on the pretense of needing to help me.

But with the way these past six months had gone, I needed those little moments of feeling good more and more desperately, and I was starting to feel that I might not be able to hold off on cutting for much longer.

192

Stephen was leaving tomorrow night – no, it would be tonight now, I reminded myself, since it was now early Thursday morning – for a business trip. He would be in St. Louis, about 800 miles away, as I had calculated it.

Every fragile bone in my body was clinging to the thought of those few precious days without him in the house.

I tried for the thousandth time to figure out where things had changed, but no matter how many times I went back over it, I could not find the place where what I had thought was imagination had turned into reality.

All I knew was that I was stuck in a hell of my own making, one I could find no way out of without sacrificing my sister. Because somewhere along the way, Stephen had taken everything from my imagination and flipped it over, making me realize that if I ever tried to say anything to Kallie about what he was doing, she would never believe me. Worse, she would know the truth: that this whole thing was really my fault.

For the hundredth time, I considered all my possible options for escape. And like always, I came back to Stephen's promise of what he would do to my sister. As the image flew unbidden into my mind, my eyes suddenly flooded with tears that I could not hold back, and as they streamed down my face, I began to shake with everything else that I was still holding tightly inside. Thinking about him doing that to Kallie made

193

me want to kill myself just so I would not have to think about it anymore.

And that was when I started to think about my one possible way of escape, one that would not involve him hurting Kallie, because I would not be around for him to hang her over my head.

Suddenly, I heard my door creak. Kallie had already been in, almost an hour ago.

No. It could not be, not now, not here. This was *my* room, *my* space.

My bedroom door opened slowly, and he came in, quietly closing it behind him and turning the lock.

He stood there by the door, watching me for several long seconds. I wanted to scream, but I was afraid to even breathe. I thought briefly of throwing myself out the window, but I was afraid to move, and besides the two-story fall would not do anything worse to me than break a bone.

And then he was across the room and kneeling on the floor beside my bed. "I came to say goodbye," he whispered. "Please come closer to me."

I did not move. He reached over, and for a moment I thought he was going to grab me; I flinched instinctively. He stopped just as his hand was hovering an inch above me. "Please. Come. Closer. To me," he repeated, again in a whisper, but much more intensely. The words were those of a request, but what he was giving was a command. I shook uncontrollably as if he had screamed in my ear, and slid closer to the edge of the bed, fighting my own movements the whole time.

"Please," I mouthed. I was ready to beg him to stop, if it would do any good.

"Please what? What is it you would like me to do, on this last night together for a few days? How would you like me to say goodbye?"

I shuddered involuntarily. "Nothing. I just want to stop."

He grinned, and again I wanted to scream. "Sorry. That's not an option." He let his hand slowly begin to touch me. "Now. Either you can tell me what you want, or I'll choose. Either way, it's ultimately your choice."

Every cell in my brain was telling me to say something, anything, but something somewhat mild, so that he would not do something completely horrible and painful. But every fiber of the rest of my being was screaming that I could not, I could *not* be a willing participant. No matter what I had done to make him do this to me, there was no way I could give him specific directions, no matter what terrors it might save me from. I refused to give him the satisfaction.

"Well, then. I'll take this to mean you want to be surprised."

I tightened my jaw and turned my head away, refusing to look at him. When he started to touch me, I shut my eyes tightly and dug my fingernails into the side of my leg, harder and harder, to give myself some other pain to focus on.

Kallie

I had always thought the house seemed quieter overall when Stephen went away to conferences, even though the only difference was during a couple of hours in the evening. But this time, with Kaedyn here, it was not quiet at all. In fact, it almost seemed noisier.

For the first time in months, Kaedyn came out of her room for more than a few minutes, and at times other than meals. She watched a movie with the girls and me, played a game on the floor with Brooke, made cookies with Celia, and read books to the girls in the library. I did not know where this girl had come from, but she was not the same girl who had been living in my house for the last five or six months. One night, I curled up in an over-stuffed leather chair in the library, across from the matching couch where Kaedyn was reading *Aesop's Fables* to the girls. And for the first time in the last six months, I really looked at my sister.

Her face was thinner, and her hoodie seemed even baggier than usual She had lost weight.

And I remembered back to a conversation with my Dad on Thanksgiving Day.

He had noticed it then. Now it was five months later, and I was finally noticing. I was the worst sister on the planet.

The part I could not figure out was *how* she could be losing weight. She ate meals with us, and while she did not always eat a lot, she always ate at least something. I had been watching her for food-avoiding habits, like dividing her food up on her plate and eating 3 peas and a bite of chicken, or making up excuses in order to skip meals, but those signals just were not there. Was it stress, then? And if so, did she have stressors other than that of losing our mom nearly nine months ago? Maybe it was all catching up with her, Mom being sick and us taking care of her and then losing the battle.

I truly was not sure what to think. But as she closed *Aesop's Fables*, I vowed to myself that I would watch her a little more closely.

It turned out, I made this decision not a moment too soon.

That night, I woke again in the night, inexplicably, only about an hour after I had fallen asleep. I lay listening for sounds of movement, wondering what it was that kept waking me.

It was midnight. I decided to check on all the girls, if

for no other reason than to ease my own mind. I slid out of bed and tugged on my robe as I slipped quietly into the hall.

Celia and Brooke were both sound asleep. I kissed their foreheads and tucked their covers tightly around their little shoulders. Brooke smiled in her sleep; Celia frowned and rolled over.

When I got to Kaedyn's room, I turned the door knob slowly, trying to remain as quiet as possible. Peering into the room, I found it enchanting that the moonlight shone through her window right across her bed, casting sparkling beams of pure white light on her quilt.

And that was when I realized Kaedyn was not in her bed.

At first, I panicked. Where could she be?

But it was only a matter of a few seconds before I heard the sound coming from the bathroom, just a few feet down the hall. To this day, I don't know why I did it, but I moved very quietly down the hall to the bathroom and stood outside the door to listen.

What I heard scared me to my core. I wondered later why I was not revolted, or angry, or why I did not totally freak out. But really all I felt was fear. Probably because it was not at all what I expected; it had never even crossed my mind as a possibility.

The next thought I had was that only something dire would drive my sister to this. But what?

Kaedyn

When I finished, I flushed the toilet, washed my hands thoroughly with soap – twice – and brushed my teeth. Then, feeling clean inside and out, I opened the door to go back to my room.

Kallie was standing there with her arms crossed over her chest.

By her stance, I immediately thought she was angry. But then I looked at her face, and I did not see anger there. Her eyes looked sad, and scared. Then she spoke, and her voice was angry; but I figured she was just trying to cover up the fact that she was really just sad and scared.

"What's going on, Kady?"

"Nothing," I replied defiantly.

"That was not 'nothing' that I just heard."

I scowled at her and turned away.

"Kady." Kallie grabbed my arm just above the elbow.

"Let go of me!" I whispered fiercely, jerking away from her.

"Tell me what is going on. Right now."

"I did tell you. Nothing. Now leave me alone." I started to move toward my bedroom.

"No, I won't," Kallie replied stubbornly, reaching for me again. "I've left you alone long enough. I'm done leaving you alone."

I ignored her and went into my room anyway. I tried to shut the door behind me, but she forced her way in behind me.

"Talk to me, Kady. Tell me what is going on."

"I don't know what you're talking about."

"You're going to tell me what's going on. Now." Her tone of voice had changed to one of demanding.

It only made it easier for me to exude anger. "No, I'm not. You're not Mom, Kallie!"

She stopped in her tracks and stared at me. Finally, after several minutes of silence, during which I assumed she was regaining her composure and calming herself so she would not start screaming at me, she spoke again. "I don't think this has anything at all to do with Mom. And if she were here and heard what I just heard in there, she would be very upset and worried. And if she thought that I knew this was going on, and just 'left you alone,' she would be very ashamed of me, and rightfully so. So, no, Kady; I'm not leaving you alone this time."

Now I was scared. How was I going to get out of this

one?

You don't have to, a tiny voice whispered in my head.

Oh yes, I did. Because there was no way Kallie could find out about what I had done, about what I was doing, to betray her.

I turned away from my sister, to hide the fear and confusion that I was sure were plain on my face. I wanted to sit on my bed, but something was stopping me; somehow I felt – however irrational – that if Kallie saw me in the bed, she would see what had happened there the night before. So I went to my desk, and sat down in the chair there.

"What is going on, Kady? Talk to me."

I put my head in my hands and shook it slowly. "I just can't – I can't think straight right now. I just want to sit down for a minute." In truth, my legs felt weak, a little bit like jell-o, and I did not think I'd be able to stand much longer without collapsing, which would really put Kallie over the edge.

Then Kallie sat on my bed. I wished she wouldn't. It made me think of all sorts of things I did not want to think about. Things that had happened there, things that he had threatened from there, things I was terrified would happen if my sister did not leave my room right this second. But instead she was sitting on the bed, with all the bad memories, as if the two could sit together for an infinite amount of time without any repercussions.

"Kady?" she said so quietly it was almost a whisper. "I'm just worried about you. You're not doing this because of Mom."

"I don't know what you're talking about."

"You know exactly what I'm talking about"

I shrugged and turned away from my sister, pulled out a book and began to read. Maybe I could just piss her off and she would leave before I told her something I shouldn't. That was the best I could hope for.

"Kady!" I could tell Kallie was exasperated. But instead of leaving like I had hoped she would, she got up off my bed and came to crouch down in front of me in the chair. She grabbed my book and threw it on the floor, then grasped my wrists and moved her face so that it was inches away from mine. "What. The hell. Is going on?!?"

I stared her down. She was not going to win this one; I was too scared. "Forget it, Kallie," I said. I could hear the hard edge in my own voice.

"No, you forget it, Kaedyn. I don't care how apathetic you sound or how mean you are to me; I'm not leaving until you talk to me."

Kallie

I wasn't sure what to do, but I knew I was not leaving without some answers. From the minute she opened the bathroom door, my sister was defiant and contentious. But I knew that was just her way of trying to push me away. There was obviously something going on that went far beyond our mother's death. Whatever it was, I was determined that my sister was not going to continue having to deal with it alone.

Despite her protests, I followed Kaedyn to her bedroom, and despite her insistence, I refused to leave. In her room, she paced back and forth in front of her bed while I tried to explain to her that Mom would not have let her deal with this alone, and she would not have wanted me to let her, either. She shrugged and turned around to actually sit at her desk like she would when she was doing schoolwork, and pulled out a book. I sat on her bed and tried to talk to her, tried to get her to talk to me, but she basically ignored me, sticking her nose in the book she had pulled out.

"Kady!" I could not help myself; I was on the verge of

raising my voice because I was so frustrated with her behavior. I knew this was wholly her intention, but knowing did not really keep me from being irritated. And my fear for my sister far outweighed any lingering worries that my girls would be woken. I left her bed and knelt in front of her, yanking her book away and throwing it on the floor. I grabbed her wrists and forced her to look at me.

"What the hell is going on???" I was done being calm, and I was done asking.

"Forget it, Kallie," she replied in a steely tone. More pushing.

"No, *you* forget it, Kaedyn," I pushed back. If I had to sleep on the floor, there was no way I would leave this room until I knew what was going on. "I don't care how apathetic you sound or how mean you are to me; I'm not leaving until you talk to me."

"Well then, you're going to be here awhile." And then my little sister murmured something that I could not quite make out, but sounded ominous.

"What?"

"I said, then you're going to be here awhile."

"And then what did you say?"

"Nothing."

"Enough with the 'nothing,' Kaedyn! I've had it!"

"You don't want to know," she replied, staring hard into my eyes. I looked back into her deep royal blue eyes. She meant what she was saying.

"I don't care, Kady. At this point, I really do not care if I'm going to want to know or not."

I could see this going back and forth all night. I was already tired just thinking about that, but I did not care. I was worried about my sister.

Kaedyn

"You don't want to know," I said, trying to sound intimidating. But I knew it would never scare my sister off. She was too much of a sister. I was racking my brain, but I could not come up with any good way to get my sister to leave my room.

"I don't care, Kady. At this point, I really do not care if I'm going to want to know or not."

I knew it. I was never going to get rid of her.

I wondered briefly how Stephen would react if he got home now, came to my room at this hour, and found Kallie and me sitting here. He would definitely think I had told her, but I was stuck on one thing. If we were together when he found us, what would he do? Would he accuse me in front of her of seducing him? Probably. Would he call me things in front of her, tell her I had forced him to be with me under threat of telling her it was all him? Probably. He knew all the psychological tricks to twist this around and manipulate it into being my fault.

But would he hurt my sister in front of me? I seriously doubted it. Would he hurt her later, afterward, once his whole manipulated story was out in the open? Not likely; because if he did, she would see the scum that he was and would realize he had made it all up. I pondered that. For her to eventually believe me and leave him would be worth enduring a period of time where she believed I had betrayed her. But that chain of events was something of a major stretch in the realm of possibility, because I still doubted that he would hurt her if she believed his twisted story.

However, I suddenly remembered, just the other night Kallie had stood up to Stephen on my behalf, which even then had given me a glimmer of hope. With that thought in mind, I realized there existed a scenario in which I could tell my sister what was going on, and which ultimately ended well.

And if there was one possible scenario, maybe there were others.

Kallie

Something changed in my sister's eyes as I sat in front
of her, holding her wrists, practically begging her to confide in
me, whatever the supposedly disastrous consequences.

"What is it?" I whispered.

Kaedyn struggled with the words. "I – I want to... I
want to – to tell you..."

I tried to urge her on with my eyes. I was afraid that if
I spoke, the spell would be broken and she would give up trying
to tell me whatever it was she was trying to tell me.

"I'm not... Stephen... the girls.... the study... Sunday..."
I could not figure out how all of her words were supposed to
fit together. "I'm – I'm a b-bad sister, Kallie," she finally
stammered.

"What?!?" I could not understand what she was talking
about. "What do you mean, Kady? You're an amazing sister!
You're great with the girls, you're loving and caring; I think
you're the best sister in the world, and anyone would be lucky
to have you as a sister."

She was shaking her head madly.

I did the only thing I could think to do. I dealt with her the way I would deal with one of my first grade students when they were so upset that they could not calm down enough to tell me what was wrong. I put my hands on both sides of her face and spoke calmly. "Take a deep breath, Kady. Take a deep breath and calm down. Shhh... it's going to be okay."

She took several deep breaths and tried again.

"S-something awful, K-Kallie."

Kaedyn's teeth began chattering as if she was standing barefoot outside in the snow.

"What is it, Kady? Tell me."

"St-Stephen. In the study. I'm – I'm s-sorry, Kallie."

"What? No, Stephen's not in the study. Stephen's not home. He's gone, remember?"

She grabbed my hands and leaned in close, her teeth still chattering like crazy. "Kal, it's supposed to be a secret. I'm not supposed to tell you. But I can't not tell you anymore."

I frowned in spite of myself. "What secret? What can't you tell me?"

She took a deep breath and spoke in the exhale. "In the study... in Stephen's study... it's not just talking, Kallie."

"What are you talking about?"

"He – he touches me. He does things. He – he acts

212

like we're doing them together but... but I don't like it. I asked him to stop but... but he – he wouldn't. He told me we – we couldn't."

I was floored. I had no words. I felt like my fingers and hands had been stomped on, they felt so numb; all the blood in my body must have rushed immediately to my head. That was the only explanation for the fact that I could no longer feel my heart beating, and that my head was pounding insanely, and that I suddenly felt like I was about to pass out on my sister's bedroom floor.

Finally, I found words. They were stuck in my dry throat, so they came out sounding like I had eaten too much of something spicy, but I forced them out. "Why would you say such a thing, Kaedyn?"

My sister's jaw dropped, and she began shaking her head crazily, her eyes wild. "No, no, Kallie, no!"

I felt a sting of sympathy for her, but then I remembered my beloved husband about whom she had said these things, and all I felt was anger. "After all I've done – after all *we've* done for you – this is how you repay our kindness? *This* is your gratitude?!? How could you say these things about my husband?? Stephen, who's never been anything but a kind brother to you, Kaedyn. How *could* you? How could you do this to me?"

"No, Kallie, wait! I'm not lying, Kallie, I'm not. Wait!"

But I could not wait. I could not stand to be in her room any longer. I could not stand to be anywhere near her. Every last ounce of worry had transformed into anger. I pushed her away from me, stumbled up from her carpeted floor, and stormed from her room. It took every ounce of willpower that I had left in me to not slam her bedroom door like a pissed off teenager.

Kaedyn

All I could think was that I had been trying to piss my sister off, and now I had succeeded.

But that hadn't gone at all how I had planned.

Or at least how I had hoped.

I had actually worried all along that she would not believe me, but those scenarios in my head had consisted of Stephen convincing Kallie that I was lying and he was telling the truth. What had just happened was worse: she had disbelieved me all on her own. She had basically called me a liar without him even being there to plant the idea in her head.

My sister hated me.

What had I done?

I left my room and went back to the bathroom. This time I locked the door behind me so that my sister could not get in. I could not be interrupted this time.

Kallie

I was so confused and disoriented by the time I returned to my own room that I wanted to grab something off the dresser – anything – and throw it as hard as I could at the mirror. And I would have screamed if it were not for my two toddlers sound asleep across the hall.

Again, it took massive amounts of restraint to avoid this teenager type behavior.

What was my sister's problem? What had caused her to make up such stories? Furthermore, where had she even gotten the idea? That was the part I was really stuck on. Where had the ideas even come from? My sister had never been a trouble maker; she had never hung out with the "bad" kids at school, had never tried to sneak out of the house, had never tried alcohol. She sure as hell had never tried drugs – I was fairly certain she had never even tried a puff of a cigarette – and the most inappropriate item of clothing she had ever worn was a skirt about three inches above her knee, and she had worn that with leggings.

And what could be her motivation for making up this kind of stories about my husband? What could she be hoping to gain through these outrageous accusations? Was she looking for attention? Was she hoping I would leave him so she could have me and the girls to herself?

Or was she trying to tell me something else?

I stared at myself in the mirror for several long minutes, silent except for the sound of my ragged breathing as I tried to find my lungs.

And then it hit me, impossible as it was: What if she was telling the truth?

As much as I did not want to, I forced myself to look myself in the eye and sit for a moment with the possibility that my sister could be telling me the truth about my husband.

No, she couldn't be. He was not capable of such a thing. He could not possibly have done those things to Kaedyn. He couldn't have. He wouldn't have.

But what if he could? What if he had?

What would it mean?

Well, for one thing, it would mean I was leaving my husband as soon as humanly possible.

Or maybe it would just mean changing the locks before he got home.

For another thing, it would mean I had some

apologizing to do, to my sister.

It also meant I had a massive mess to sort out and try to fix.

I shook my head. Was I going crazy? This was my husband I was thinking about. I had known him longer than Kaedyn had been alive. I had loved him and he had loved me for fourteen long years.

Or had he?

As my brain scanned quickly back over the years, I found myself second guessing his love for me. Had it all been an act? Had he been lying? If so, what was his motivation?

And now I was back to my original question. Motivation. Why would Kaedyn lie about this? I could come up with no plausible reason.

Still, weighing the likelihood of my sister lying to me now against the possibility my husband had lied to me for our whole life together was difficult, to say the least. Besides, Kaedyn had been just a baby when we had started dating, the same age Brooke was now. Thinking about what my sister had just told me... I almost threw up in my own lap.

Then a thought hit me as hard as if I had slammed my head into a brick wall.

What if he had touched one of the girls?

No, I told myself, it was impossible. They were his own

daughters, his own flesh and blood. He would never do anything to hurt them, especially not like that.

I barely made it to my bathroom before I threw up for real this time. Afterwards, as I was sitting on the floor with my forehead resting against the cool ceramic of the toilet, I suddenly thought of my sister and wondered if she was back in her bathroom. If someone did a cutaway of my house, would they see mirror images of the two of us right now, on opposite ends of the same distress?

This would certainly explain her strange behavior over the last few months. This would more than explain why I had caught her making herself throw up — and by the way, I was certain this was far from the first time she had done it. I knew without a doubt now that she was the reason I had been waking inexplicably in the middle of the night. Why would she have hidden that from me if she were lying now?

Who was more likely to lie to me, my sister or my husband?

Then I realized something. My husband hadn't outright lied to me yet, at least not to my face. But if he *were* here, what would he have said?

If he did lie to me, would I know?

Maybe I would now.

It had to be him. It had to be. My emotions were all

tangled up, not wanting to believe that my husband was capable of this but also not wanting to believe my sister would make up stories like this. It wasn't like she was lying about staying out past curfew; she had just told me that my husband had touched her, inappropriately, several times over the course of... had she even given me a time frame?

I had to ignore my emotions right now and think about the facts. And the facts told me that Kaedyn had to be telling me the truth.

Pieces suddenly clicked into place. The fact that the longer she talked to Stephen, the less she talked to me. My own discomfort every time they went behind the closed office door. The day I had walked in on them, when Stephen had been in a hurry for me to leave, and Kaedyn had looked so desperately vulnerable sitting on his couch. And just the other night, when Stephen had snapped at her at the dinner table, and the look in her eyes when she had stared him down, and the way she had glued herself to my side until I had gone to bed. It was gut-wrenching. As thoughts of Stephen touching Kaedyn flashed unbidden into my mind, I vomited again.

I had accused my sister of lying to me out of shock and anger, but now I realized the anger was not toward her.

It was directed at myself.

Because if she was telling the truth, then it had all

happened right under my nose.

I quickly scanned back through my memory to try to figure out how long it could have been going on. The two of them had been "talking" in the study for at least four or five months, but I could not trust my memory on the time frame. And would that matter anyway? Could it have been going on even longer than that?

I sighed, got to my feet, rinsed my mouth, and washed my face. I needed to find Kaedyn.

Kaedyn

In the bathroom, I unzipped my jeans and pushed them down to my knees as I knelt on the plush bath mat in front of the sink. I dug into the drawer under the sink where I kept all of my things and found my shaving razor. I took a brand new cartridge out of the package, and using my fingernails, pulled apart the plastic and freed the blades from the casing. They spilled onto the mat, their shiny surfaces sending scattered bits of light onto the ceiling and walls and my shoulder. I wrapped three of the four individual blades carefully in a tissue and took the other gingerly in my fingers. Then I pressed the corner of the blade into the soft white skin on the slight inside of my lower thigh, just above my knee.

As I slowly cut the tender skin, watching red beads of blood form along the thin line I was making, I thought about what would happen next.

My sister would tell Stephen about what I had tried to tell her.

He would be angry. And sickeningly pleased, because it

223

would give him an excuse to do more – or worse – things.

He would laugh it off with her, tell her that I must have misunderstood his intentions as we sat and talked about my mother's death. He would probably tell her that it was not uncommon for someone dealing with grief to form a disillusioned bond in their mind with a counselor, someone who seemed to be the only person who understood what they were going through. He would promise her that she had nothing to worry about, and all the while he would be making plans in his head about when and where and what he would do to punish me. And then he would tell my sister that he would stop talking alone with me and refer me to a therapist, probably one in his office. He might even say something to the effect that he should not have tried to talk with me; he should have found me a therapist right away.

God help me.

If he sent me to someone else, he would tell them that I had made up stories about us and told them to my sister. He could easily make me out to be a crazy and delusional pathological liar.

It sounded like one of the well-written psychological thriller movies that actually scared me because they were so frighteningly realistic. My life was about to become script fodder.

The only thing I was not sure about was whether or not he would hurt Kallie, or the girls. He had threatened to hurt Kallie if I told, but I wondered if maybe he really wouldn't hurt her, as long as he could convince her that it was all in my head – if he could continue his perfect life here and still keep hurting me.

I did not know what to do.

I could run away, but they would eventually find me. I had nowhere to go.

I could call my dad, but I did not really want to drag him into this. And besides, that was nearly as big a gamble as telling Kallie had been; he would never know whether to believe me or Kallie, especially if Stephen had all kinds of psychological terms to use against me.

I did know one thing for sure: if I stayed here, things were just going to get worse.

But I did not know where to go. I needed to escape, and suddenly I knew there was only one way to do it.

When I looked down at my leg, there were rivulets of blood running down and dripping onto the floor. I had intended to now take the blade to the inside of my wrists and make my escape, to get myself out of here and never have to come back.

But the pain that shot through my entire leg was

unnaturally comforting, almost healing.

The rush I got from the physical pain was just as consuming as it always was. I needed that feeling again. I drew the blade back over my thigh, this time relishing the feeling, losing myself in the sharp, centering pain.

I was making the third cut when I heard the knock on the door and heard my sister's voice.

"Kady?"

"Go away." I was amazed at how calmly I was able to say it, quietly and without anger or panic.

"Kady, I need to talk to you. Please open the door."

"I can't talk to you right now, Kallie. In fact, I don't think I can talk to you anymore ever."

"Kady..." She sounded like she was crying. "I'm sorry," she whispered against the seam where the door latched closed.

I blinked, staring at the blood gushing from my leg. She was sorry?

"What do you mean?"

"I mean I'm sorry. I'm sorry I didn't believe you. I'm sorry I called you a liar. Please open the door so I can talk to you."

I glanced up to reassure myself that the door was indeed locked. "Just a minute." Then I looked around wildly for something to staunch the blood flow and keep my sister from discovering what I had just done. I found a clean wash cloth in my drawer, folded it in half, and pressed it against my leg, holding it there while I pulled my pants up over it. It was a bit bulky, but it was all I had right now. I could bandage it up properly later. I grabbed a handful of toilet paper and mopped up the blood from the floor, then flushed it down the toilet.

Quickly wrapping the blade in the tissue with the others, I tucked the little package in the pocket of my jeans as I stood up. Then I unlocked the door and cracked it open. Kallie stood there, looking worried. I did not know what to say, so I just waited for her to speak.

"Can we talk?" she finally said.

"Sure," I replied, but made no motion to move.

"Can I come in, or do you want to go somewhere else?"

I shrugged.

My sister reached through the crack, pushing the door open slightly more, and grabbed my hand. I did not resist when she pulled me from the bathroom, and into her arms for a tight embrace. Then she tugged me down the hall toward my bedroom.

"Wait." I pulled back on her arm when we approached my door. "Please. Not in my room. Don't make me talk about it in there."

I could see my sister's mind processing the possible

227

reasons for my resistance. I could tell she wanted to ask, but she just nodded and turned to retreat down the hall in the opposite direction, to the library.

Kallie

It did not sound like Kaedyn was throwing up when I got to the hall outside her bathroom door, but when I thought I had finally convinced her to open the door, she still made me wait. I could hear her moving around in there, but I wasn't sure what she was doing. I silently tried the door knob, but it was locked, as I had suspected. It was worth a try. Then I heard the toilet flush, and the door opened, just enough that she could peer out at me.

"Can we talk?"

"Sure." But she did not move to come out of the bathroom; she was clearly waiting for me to set the stage. I thought for a second.

"Can I come in? Or do you want to go somewhere else?"

It was barely perceptible from where I was standing in the dark hallway, but Kaedyn shrugged just slightly. I took that as the sign that she wanted me to lead. So I reached in and gently took her hand, hugged her tightly for a minute, then started to lead her down the hall toward her bedroom.

"Wait." She pulled back hard on my arm. "Please don't make me talk about it in there."

Dear God, what had he done to her? And in her bedroom? I had to fight back against the nauseating feelings rising in my chest again.

Quickly switching gears, I thought through the rooms of the house. I could not take her to my room; she would only think of that as the space I shared with him. So I took her to the library, where we sat together on the black leather couch.

I watched my little sister for a moment as she pulled her knees to her chest and wrapped her arms around her legs, pressing her eyes against her knees. I had a sudden flash of a memory of her sitting like this, on the floor in front of the television, in her sleeper pajamas, the ones with the feet. I had just gotten home from college for the summer. I was nineteen; Kaedyn was six, almost seven. She missed me so much when I was away that when I got home, she would wake me early every morning for nearly a month. I would make her waffles, and we would watch cartoons together.

That was the summer I had gotten engaged.

Kaedyn had been so young, and she hadn't understood. Oh, she liked Stephen well enough; he was over for dinner all the time, and often spent weekends with us. He knew how to tickle Kaedyn in just such a way as to get the biggest giggles out of her. But when I had told her we were getting married, she had cried and cried; she had thought she was losing me.

What had I done?

Finally, I found the courage to ask for the answer. "Tell me," I whispered.

Kaedyn swallowed hard. "Are you sure?"

I knew what she meant. Was I sure I was going to believe her this time. Was I sure I was not going to accuse her of lying to me. Was I sure I wanted to hear it.

I nodded. "Yes. Please tell me."

She took a deep breath. "I – I wish I could tell you when it started, but I really don't know. I've tried so hard to remember... to – to figure out when it first happened... but..." She looked at me almost pleadingly, begging me with her eyes to understand. "But I just don't know. I think... I think it was around Christmas... it was sometime after the first time when he asked me if I needed to talk. He told me that if I – if I needed to talk to let him know. It was sometime after that..."

I nodded, working hard to keep my face impassive, silently urging her to continue talking.

"He would sit next to me on the couch. He would touch my back and my neck and my shoulders, then my arms. Then he would touch my legs. Then he... he would touch me...

other places." Her eyes met mine again, and one tear ran down her cheek.

I reached out with one finger to gently brush it away.

She took a steadying breath and continued. "The first time when he... when he touched me... like that... I told him I didn't want to talk anymore. He said – he said I didn't have a choice anymore. He said if I stopped coming, he – he would tell you what I had done. He... he said he would do things to you... to hurt you."

More tears began to pour down her face. I kept still, afraid to startle her, and my own eyes filled with tears.

"He said... he said..."

"What, Kady?" I whispered. "What else did he say?" I was afraid to know anymore, but I knew I needed to know, and my sister needed me to know.

Her brow was deeply creased with worry as her eyes searched mine. I moved across the couch and took my sister in my arms, holding her tightly and gently stroking her hair. "It's okay, Kady. You can tell me. He's not going to hurt you anymore; I promise. I won't let him hurt you again."

"Kallie," Kaedyn's voice was so soft I had to strain to hear her. "He said you wouldn't believe me." And then she burst into tears, unable to hold back anymore. "He said you would – you would see what a – a slut I really am, and that you

232

wouldn't... you wouldn't believe me."

I held my sister even more tightly. Anguish gripped my heart. I had made his threats and her fears come true. Regardless of how short the time was and how quickly I had seen how wrong I was, I had given real weight to his threats. "I'm so, so sorry, Kady." I did not know what else to say. In truth, words could not capture how sorry I was. I wished I could go back and take it all back, think things through before responding to her accusations. "I'm so sorry."

Kaedyn

I thought I would feel better after I told Kallie, but I still felt as worried and anxious as ever. I was sure that once Stephen got home, he would find a way to convince her that I was lying, and I would be back in hell. My sister must have read some of my worry on my face.

"It will be okay," she assured me for about the twenty-seventh time in ten minutes.

I nodded, unconvinced.

"I know," she said softly. "I know that he told you I wouldn't believe you. I'm sorry for saying that I didn't. But I do, Kady, I do believe you. And it's going to be okay. He's not going to hurt you anymore, I promise."

"Okay." Then I thought of something else. "What about you, Kallie? When he finds out I told you and he can't convince you I'm lying, he'll hurt you."

"No, Sweetie. He's not going to hurt anyone else anymore. He's done with that. I promise."

"What are you going to do?"

Kallie took a deep breath and rose from the couch. "Well, I don't suppose I'm going to get you to go to bed and get some sleep?"

I shook my head. I was way too wired to sleep. And I did not have the energy to even try to go into my room, let alone sleep in my own bed.

"What if I come to bed with you?" Kallie asked, as if reading my mind.

I thought about it. "Maybe."

Then Kallie frowned. "Wait a minute. Where have you been sleeping the last few nights?"

I took a deep breath and met her questioning gaze. Then I turned and reached down between the end of the couch and the wall; there was about a foot and a half of space there, and I pulled out the blanket and pillow I had been stashing there. She had guessed right: I had not been able to feel safe back in my own bed after the night he had come to my room.

Then it was my turn to frown. "You haven't been checking in on me?"

My sister shrugged. "The first two nights I didn't wake up."

I felt my features twist up in confusion. Weird.

Kallie shook her head as if clearing her thoughts. "I won't ask now, but – but sometime... I want you to tell me about... about that." I chewed on my lower lip. I didn't know if I would be able to tell her that part. "Let's go. First thing tomorrow I'm calling the police, the locksmith, the doctor, and the attorney, in that order; but there's nothing else to be done tonight. Let's at least try to get some rest."

I nodded, exhausted and resigned. Then all of her words caught up with my ears.

"Wait. Police? Doctor? Lawyer? What?"

Kallie sighed. "We'll talk about it tomorrow, Kade. Now is not the time. I should have thought before I spoke."

My jaw tightened, but Kallie was right. It was not a good time to get into an argument about whether to call the police or not.

Even though my room was flooded with bright moon light, Kallie turned on the lamp beside my bed. I was thankful for that. There was no such thing as too much light right now. In my twin bed, Kallie curled up next to me, but being in that bed still made me feel sick to my stomach. After only a few minutes, I could no longer stand it.

"Where are you going?" Kallie asked when I got out of bed.

"My stomach hurts."

"So where are you going?" She was going to make me admit it.

"Just to the bathroom. I'll be back in a minute." I tried to make it sound casual. Instead it just sounded... stupid.

"No way, Kady. You're done with that."

"I feel sick, Kallie. It's not like I can help it."

She looked around the room. Then she got up and left the room, returning after a minute with clean sheets and blankets from the hall linen closet. She spread them on the floor, put new pillowcases on my pillows, and dropped them down on top of the blankets, tossing the old pillowcases back onto my bed.

"Here. We'll sleep on the floor. It will be just like when you were little and we had our little sleepovers."

I looked from my sister to the makeshift pallet, then back to my sister. Maybe it could work. "Okay." I curled up next to my sister under the quilt, and she slipped her arm around my shoulders. I started to feel better after a few minutes of lying there. The sheets smelled clean, and my sister was there. Still, I had a hard time falling asleep.

"Still awake?" I had no idea how much time had passed when my sister's soft voice in the dark silence surprised me.

"Yes," I whispered.

"Want to talk about it?"

"I – I don't know," I replied honestly.

"Okay. Well, it's okay if you do. I'm here."

I nodded against her arm. My mind was racing, and I was having a hard time keeping up with all the times and places and memories that my thoughts were flitting back and forth to and from. It was starting to make me feel dizzy on the inside. I had no idea how I could even begin to put any of it into words for Kallie.

I was lying on my stomach with my arms wrapped around my pillow and my chin resting on the pillow, staring at the closet door and struggling to come up with the words to explain to Kallie what had happened.

Suddenly a memory, like a quick snap shot, drifted through my brain. I did not know where it had come from or what had made me think of it, but I struggled to grab it and hold onto it so I could remember all of it.

The memory was of me sitting in my huge toy box, peeking over the top of it. I was hiding from someone, but I could not remember who. I had an odd sense of déjà vu.

Then I remembered I had already tried to work through this memory once before. Pulling away from my sister, I got up off the blankets and went to my desk.

"What are you doing?" Kallie asked.

Ignoring her, I dug through the bottom left side drawer, pushing aside all the obstacles I had placed there to deter anyone who might try to be nosy: notebooks, sketch pads, a pencil case, and a ream of computer paper. In the bottom of the drawer, all the way at the back, I found my journal. I pulled it out and returned to the blanket. My sister was watching me with curiosity plain on her face as I began to search through my journal.

"I'm trying to remember something," I explained. "Just give me a minute."

My sister nodded and watched me silently as I scanned the pages in the book. I finally found what I was looking for.

It was just a general entry, one of those memories that had jumped into my mind shortly after Mom died, and I had written it down simply so that I would never forget it again.

When I was a baby, I had this toy box that was handmade for me by the husband of one of my mom's friends. It was huge, probably three feet wide by five feet long, and at least two and a half feet deep. Mom put the toy box in my closet, because it was so big that there wasn't any room for it out in the main part of my bedroom. Even as a toddler, I loved that toy box being in the closet, because I could play in there, and it was kind of like a secret little fort. The first time I realized that I could actually hide in there, I was about two years old. It was a time I was playing in there with my tea set, and my mom came to find me for dinner. When I heard her

coming, I stopped talking to myself, and waited for her to find me. She looked for me for the longest time, calling my name but not knowing where I was. I thought it was so funny that I finally couldn't hold in my giggles anymore. My mom found me, and we laughed together, my mom teasing me about hiding from her. After that, I never could hide from her there again, not that I ever wanted to.

But I did learn that I could hide there from other people. One time, only a few days after I turned seven, I was playing in there with my dolls. I heard someone come into my sister Kallie's room, which was connected to my room by a door just outside of my closet. I stayed quiet, because I wanted to know who it was. I knew it wasn't Kallie, because the footsteps didn't sound like hers. I remember peeking over the edge to see if I could see who it was. It was my brother Kurt and Kallie's boyfriend Stephen. I wondered what they were doing in Kallie's room, especially without her, so I stayed quiet and kept watching. Once I had to duck back down into the toy box because Stephen turned around a little bit, and I was afraid for a moment that he was going to see me. He didn't though, and he and Kurt kept talking.

Kurt said, "In there. That's where she keeps her

stuff."

And Stephen said, "Thanks, Bud. She's going to really love this surprise. Thanks for your help."

Kurt said, "No problem," and he sounded like he was grinning. He was proud that he had helped Stephen plan some big surprise for Kallie. Then Kurt left, and Stephen stayed in the room.

After a minute or two, I looked up over the edge of the toy box again, to see what Stephen was doing. He was digging around in Kallie's dresser drawers, but I couldn't tell which drawers or exactly what he was doing. He took something out of his jacket pocket. Then he dug around in the drawers some more, then he put something into his jacket pocket. Then he suddenly shut the drawers and turned to leave. I ducked down again really fast. I was so afraid again that he had seen me. I remember holding my hand over my mouth so that I wouldn't breathe loudly enough for him to hear me. I stayed there for a very long time, because I wanted to be sure he was gone. When my mom came to get me for supper, I was finally sure Stephen hadn't seen me.

For some reason, this incident bothered me for days and days, even weeks, after it happened. I wanted to tell Kallie about it, but I kept reminding myself of the

242

conversation Stephen and Kurt had exchanged, that this was some big surprise for Kallie, and if I told her, I would ruin the great surprise. So I never told her, even though I wanted to for a very long time. Then, when weeks went by and I didn't hear anything from Kallie about a special surprise from Stephen, I started to worry again. What had he been doing in there?

I eventually convinced myself that the surprise was meant for Kallie only, and that I was never supposed to know about it. Kallie seemed okay, and it wasn't too long after this that she announced to us she was marrying Stephen. Maybe it had something to do with that. I was never sure, and even though I always wished I could have found a way to talk to Kallie about it, I eventually convinced myself not to worry about it anymore.

When I finally finished reading, I took a deep breath and blinked my eyes several times, as if I had barely dared to breathe or blink while reading the entry. Then I re-read the memory written in my own words for the first time six months ago; it was much easier the second time, and when I finished, I looked up at my sister. Did I dare let her read it? I had felt a strange pull to tell her about this for nine years now. Would she be mad at me? Even if she was, would it be worth it if she could shed some light on the memory?

"May I?" she asked, interrupting my internal struggle.

"If you promise not to be mad. It's something that happened a long time ago. I forgot about it until recently. Please don't be mad that I didn't tell you sooner."

"I promise."

I handed her the book.

Kallie

As I read my sister's journal entry, I felt as though a blanket of sheer ice was being draped around me. I grew very cold, and as I read the entry for the third time, my vision began to blur.

"No," I whispered softly, incredulously.

I could not believe what I was reading. I could feel that my jaw was hanging open, but I could not find the muscles to close my mouth. Finally, I forced my head up so I could look at my sister, who was watching me with a worried look cast over her features. I realized that the pained look on my face was probably causing her even more worry; I remembered suddenly that she had been afraid that I would be angry with her after reading what she had written.

"No," I said again quietly, pulling her into my arms. "It's not you, it's..."

She held onto me tightly, as if she was afraid of losing me. A shiver ran through me as I realized how close she must have thought she had gotten to losing me; I was not going to let her come that close ever again.

"It's not you, Sweetie, I promise. It's just that..." I motioned to the book. "This... it's..." I stopped. Should I tell her the truth behind what she had written? Was it fair to add that to all the things that were already on her mind? Would it just make things worse?

"What?" Kaedyn demanded.

"Nothing, it's... just... you have a really good memory."

"Huh-uh, Kallie. You *know*. You know what he was doing." Her tone was accusing, and rightfully so. The recognition of sororal lying apparently went both ways.

I pulled back and looked into her eyes. Despite everything that had happened, they were still filled with innocence. She was learning, maybe for the first time, how horrible people could be; but I still didn't think all of the manipulation that was involved had sunk in for her yet. That is, I understood enough of psychology to know that Stephen had to have used a variety of types and levels of manipulation in order to keep her quietly in his grasp. I shuddered. I just was not sure that now was the time to introduce her to the actual depths of the possibilities of manipulation.

Especially when I had not had time to process it myself.

Not that it took much for me to understand what had happened. It was processing everything that had happened as a result that was going to take me some time.

At least five minutes.

I wished he would come home early. I wished he would walk in the door right now. I needed to scream, and I wanted to scream at him. I wanted to tell him all the thoughts that were racing through my mind about him and what an absolutely horrible person he was. I wanted to tell him all the thoughts that were racing through my mind about myself and what an idiot I was to have ever believed anything he had ever told me. And that was just for what he had done to me.

For what he had done to my sister, I wanted to get a baseball bat and beat the hell out of him.

And God help me if I found out he had ever touched the girls. That would just put me right over the edge, and I would probably end up in jail for manslaughter.

"Kallie?" Kaedyn's voice was tentative. I looked up at her again.

"Sorry."

"What's going on?"

"Nothing."

"Kallie." Her tone was reproving.

I sighed. She was not going to let me get away with lying to her any more than I had let her get away with lying to me. "I don't know where to start. It's a very... twisted... story.

247

I haven't even comprehended all of it yet."

She just looked at me. "I want to know what I saw. I want to know what I — what I've done, what I've caused by not telling you all these years that something about that bothered me."

"No, Kady." I hugged her tightly again, stroking her light blond hair away from her face. "You have not caused anything. It was him. He did it; he caused it. He is the only one, do you understand that?"

But Kaedyn just held me tightly around the waist, and within moments I could feel tears soaking the front of my tee shirt. She was soon shaking as the sobs that had been a long time coming began to rack her body. I just held her and ran my fingers through her hair.

"You were just a little girl, Kady. You couldn't have possibly known that he was doing anything wrong. You couldn't have possibly known that what you heard him say to Kurt was a lie."

"Yeah, that would be easy to believe if I had left my stupidity in my childhood," Kaedyn choked against the tears.

I pulled back and held her at arm's length by her shoulders. "What are you talking about, Kaedyn?" I had my strong suspicions, but I figured this was as good a time as any to get her feelings of guilt and self blame out in the open so she could start to deal with them.

She bit down hard on her bottom lip. The tears continued to pour down her face.

"Tell me, Kady. What did you mean?"

She took a deep, ragged breath. "It's my fault, okay, Kallie?!?" I frowned, not at her words, but at her tone. It was angry, defensive. I let her keep talking. "You might as well know now, because as soon as he gets home you're going to hear it from him anyway, and then you're going to hate me, so you might as well know now. It was *my* fault, Kallie. I went to his office when he told me to. I didn't tell you what was going on, even though I wanted to. I let him do all those things he did to me. It was my fault, and you might as well hear it from me and not him."

Using the sleeve of my long sleeved tee shirt, I brushed away the tears from her cheeks. "No, Kady, I know it was not your fault. He told you he would hurt me, remember? He told you I wouldn't believe you. He scared you into not resisting him, into not escaping; but that is his fault, not yours."

She shook her head, and the tears started to fall again. I sighed softly. I knew I did not have a chance of convincing her. It was going to take someone a lot more skilled than I to help her. In fact, it was going to take someone a lot more skilled than most therapists, thanks to Stephen.

But I was stuck on one of her phrases from her outburst.

"Kady?" I asked when she had calmed down again. "What does 'all those things he did to me' mean?"

She swiped at her tears and gave me a quizzical look. "Before, you told me he touched you. Just now, you said 'I let him do all those things he did to me.' What things did he do to you, Kady?"

Kaedyn squeezed her eyes tightly shut, breathing shallowly. When she opened her eyes again, it took a minute for me to identify the look in her eyes. It was embarrassment.

I forced myself to ask the question I was terrified of knowing the answer to. "Did he... rape you?" My voice was so soft even I could barely hear it.

Kaedyn shuddered and pressed her eyes tightly into her knees again. I felt helpless as I watched my sister collapse in on herself. I knew what I was seeing was an affirmative answer to my question.

"How many times?" I whispered.

She began to shake her head back and forth slowly. "I... I don't... I don't know. I can't... I can't remember."

I sucked in a deep breath. He had raped her so many times she couldn't even remember them all? Suddenly I didn't want to wait for him to get home. I wanted to get on a plane, fly to Saint Louis, and strangle him in his hotel bed with my bare hands. I looked down to see that my hands were trembling violently in my lap. "I'm so sorry, Sweetie," I said, reaching over to gently rub her arm. She flinched slightly at the touch, and I winced. Her pain was palpable in the air. I wanted to hold her tightly and just absorb all of her anguish.

"I'm sorry," I whispered. I took her in my arms again, and we lay back down on the pallet on the floor. I cradled her head on my shoulder and held her close for several silent minutes. "Was there anything else?"

Kaedyn's hands clenched and unclenched anxiously.

"I'm sorry, Honey. I don't mean to make you think you have to talk to me about things you don't want to," I said softly. "I'm just... I'm just very angry at Stephen, and very worried about you, and it makes me want to know everything."

She nodded against my shoulder. "I know," she whispered. "I just... I don't know how to describe the... the other things."

We lay quietly in the soft lamp light for what seemed like a very long time. I had no idea what time it was, and I was amazed that my girls were still sound asleep through all the emotion that was going on just down the hall from their bedroom.

My thoughts drifted back over our last few words. Dear

God, what had he done to her? I wondered, not for the first time tonight. Whatever he had done to her was embarrassing for her to even think about; they were things that her innocent mind classified separately from rape, and went beyond touching. I shuddered as the possibilities passed through my mind. Then I began to shake with anger. How could he? How could he do those things to her? Forget the fact that he was married and he had betrayed me by doing such things; she was sixteen years old, for God's sake! I found myself wanting to scream again.

"Kallie?" Kaedyn's whisper broke the silence.

"Yeah?" I forced myself to calm down.

"Will you please tell me what – what it was I saw him doing... that day?"

I sighed with the inevitability of it all. She wasn't going to forget; she was going to keep asking me until I told her. Besides, I reasoned, she kind of deserved to know, given all that she had been through. Maybe it would help her realize that none of this was her fault; he was a manipulating creep who had orchestrated every piece of this twisted puzzle.

"You need to understand, none of this is your fault. You simply saw something you did not understand. He knew exactly what he was doing, and he was doing it intentionally. I need you to tell me that you understand that."

Kaedyn

I weighed Kallie's words carefully. I knew what she was saying was true; at least, I knew it in my head. But my emotions were telling me otherwise. Still, I knew I had to tell her I understood in order to hear the story. So I nodded.

"We had these two friends that we had been friends with since high school. Nathan and Melody Brady. They were brother and sister. Mel was my age, and Nate was a year older than me, a year younger than Stephen."

"I remember them."

Kallie nodded. "They hung out at our house a lot. Well, during spring break that year, we all hung out for pretty much the entire week. Stephen wanted us to all go on a trip, and Mel loved the idea too, but neither Nate nor I were big on the party scene, so we both objected. That was probably the start of what got Stephen riled up. So we ended up just hanging out the whole week; watching movies, mostly; we went to the amusement park once, and out to the movie theater a few times. By the end of spring break, Stephen had it in his head that Nate and I were... doing something behind his back. We got into a big fight about it; Stephen all but accused me of cheating on him. I left to go back to school feeling defeated, certain that he and I were going to be finished before too much longer."

I listened intently. I had never known about this fight.

"So imagine my surprise when the semester ended, and he showed up to drive me home. He apologized, said he didn't know what had gotten into him, but he knew I would never cheat on him, especially with Nate. I reassured him that I wouldn't cheat on him with anyone, and that Nate and I were only friends; I never even spent time with Nate alone – we were only together when the four of us hung out. We got home, and things were fine.

"Then one day, probably near the middle of July, Melody called me, practically in tears. She said she needed to talk to me right away. Stephen was at home with me, of course, and I told Mel to come over. She rushed over; when she saw Stephen was there, she asked if we could talk alone. She sat in my bedroom, telling me in a panic how she had found something in Nate's bedroom and didn't know what to make of it. It took me awhile to drag it out of her, but I finally did."

Kallie paused. I could feel her looking at me, even though I couldn't see her eyes because I was still snuggled up to her side. "What?" I asked. "What was it?"

My sister took a deep breath. "It was a pair of my underwear."

"What??" I pulled away from my sister and looked at her in shock.

"Yeah. I was stunned. At first I thought she was accusing me of messing around with Nate, but then she made it clear that she knew I would never cheat on Stephen, and she was just as confused about it as I was. Then *I* began to panic. If Stephen found out about this, there was no doubt that he would think I was cheating on him with Nate, especially given the incident after spring break. So I explained to Mel that Stephen and I had already fought once because he had once suspected I was fooling around with Nate, and I begged her not to tell anyone about this. Of course, she promised; she was my best friend. We... well, based on the... um... evidence... we concluded that Nate must have a crush on me that he had been keeping hidden because of Stephen, and that maybe he had stolen it one time when they were at our house. We concocted a story for Mel, in case Nate noticed it was missing, but he never did mention it to her.

"That was the end of it. Except..." Kallie's voice trailed off, and I could tell she was remembering something else.

"What?" I asked, unable to hold back my own impatience.

"Well, it's just... It was exactly a week later that he asked me to marry him. I – I had thought about the incident when he asked me, and I remember thinking that if I said yes, he would know that no matter what, I loved him, and I had never and would never cheat on him."

Kallie looked at me with an incredulous look on her face. "I mean... I would have said yes anyway." Was she trying to convince herself? I couldn't tell for sure.

For my part, I was trying to put it all together and make sense of it. I thought back through what I had seen from my hiding place in the toy box. He had been digging through her drawers; he had stuck something in his pocket. Of course. But then...?

I propped myself up on one elbow. "He – he left something there, Kallie. In your drawer... he left something in your drawer."

Kallie nodded but did not say anything.

"Kallie, come on." I could tell she was turning it over in her head. "What was it?"

My sister sighed. "It was the 'evidence' Mel and I had that brought us to the conclusion that Nate had stolen the underwear."

"Kallie." I was exasperated. "You can't protect me from everything."

"Apparently, I can't protect you from anything." My sister's voice was raw with contempt.

"*Ka*llie. What was it?"

She sighed loudly, making it perfectly clear that she did not want to give me this information. "It was a picture of the four of us from spring break. Stephen's face had been slightly scratched out. Not violently or anything, just... kind of scratched over. The picture was off to the side of the drawer, as if it had been dropped and just slid down there. Mel and I found it when we went back to the drawer to investigate."

I frowned. Why had my sister been reluctant to tell me about the picture? "You're not telling me something," I mused.

Kallie rolled her eyes at me.

"Oh just tell me. I think we're past all that now."

"Almost."

"What?"

"Well... there are still things I want to know."

I chewed the inside of my lip. "I'll try, Kallie," I said quietly. "But I can't promise I'll be able to... to say it out loud."

My sister reached out and ran one finger down my cheek. "I know. It's going to be okay, Kady."

I nodded. Then I backed up to the bit of information I

257

was still searching for. "There was something else in the drawer, wasn't there? What was it?"

"It was a small bottle of my lotion, half empty," Kallie finally said quietly. "It was a brand new bottle; I had just bought it the day before. I hadn't even opened it yet."

I felt like my brain was stuck. Lotion? What did that have to do with anything?

My face was frozen in a puzzled frown. My sister held my gaze for several long minutes as she waited for me to try to work it out. It wasn't coming.

Kallie laughed a small amused and frustrated laugh. "You're so naïve, Kady."

I scowled at her. "I am not."

She just shook her head at me in a resigned sort of way. "The lotion was intended to make me think someone – Nate – had been... doing something... to himself... while he was going through my drawer."

My eyes widened in surprised realization and my cheeks blazed. "Oh."

Kallie giggled at me again. "Anyway, it worked. That was exactly what Mel and I thought, and why it was so easy for us to believe Nate had... you know... taken the underwear."

I nodded. It was all starting to make sense.

Twisted, sick sense, but sense all the same.

258

I had been trying to avoid these thoughts for months, but with this new knowledge, I could not keep the thoughts away any longer. My brain did a flash forward from then to now, and I could feel my facial features contorting with disgust as I thought about all that had transpired over the years. Kallie had married Stephen within the next year after that had happened. Married people... did things. They had been married for eight years and had two children. How many times had they... in eight years? How many times had Stephen touched my sister? How many times had he done those things he had done to me, and how many times had my sister enjoyed it?

I couldn't help it; my stomach was starting to heave. I sat up quickly and grabbed the nearby waste basket and threw up in it.

Kallie sat up and moved toward me worriedly. "What is it?" she asked, her voice and eyes laced with concern.

I threw up again. When I knew I was done, I got up. "Just going to brush my teeth," I assured my sister. "I'll be right back."

Kallie

I was on pins and needles, fighting the urge to count the minutes she was gone, until Kaedyn came back from the bathroom.

When she returned, she lay down and crawled back into my arms, pulling the blankets with her. I held her, trying to warm her freezing hands.

"What just happened, Kady?" I finally asked.

"I just... I thought of something. It made me sick. I couldn't help it."

"Kady." I tried to make it plain in my voice that this hiding stuff was no longer an option.

"Please, Kallie, don't make me tell you."

I just held her silently. I did not answer her either way. I could tell by the way she was fighting it that deep down inside she really wanted to tell me. I was right; she finally spoke, albeit in a whisper.

"I just thought about... about how many times you and Stephen must have... in the past eight years."

261

I nodded. "I thought maybe that was it. Don't worry; I've thought about that too."

"You have?"

"Of course. It's natural. Sex is something you're supposed to pledge to only your spouse. It's only natural that that part of this whole thing would cross my mind about a million times." It was hard for me to say it so candidly, but I felt strongly that my sister needed to know that the whole "secret" part of all this was his doing, not hers and certainly not mine. "And it's only natural that you would think about it," I added. "I'm your sister, and I'm married. It's not like you didn't know all those years that we were having sex. It's no secret that married people do."

Kaedyn nodded, processing this statement. "Can I ask you something?"

"Anything."

"Do you... I mean... tell me honestly." I nodded. "Do you feel any... any anger or anything toward me... you know... because I'm the one he..."

I sighed. "No, Kady," I said softly. "You did not do anything wrong. I am very angry at Stephen, both for what he has done to you and for what he has thereby done to me. It's a very complicated web of thought, but all of my anger is completely and solely directed at him. He's very lucky he isn't here right now."

Kaedyn nodded again. She still seemed to be deep in thought.

"What else?" I asked gently when she had been silent for several long minutes.

"I don't know," she said hesitantly.

"It's okay, Kady. You can ask me anything."

"I don't know... It's just... I don't know."

I gave her shoulders a little squeeze, and she tightened her arms around my waist. "Do you want to tell me more about it?"

"Yes... And no."

"I can understand that. I'm here for whatever you need, okay?"

We lapsed into silence again. About twenty minutes had passed when I lifted my head slightly to glance over my sister at the clock; it read three twenty-seven.

Kaedyn had finally dozed off. I could not imagine how exhausted she must have been. I looked around the room. When had Stephen started coming into her room? For how long had she felt unsafe in her own bedroom? I sighed, forcing down the anger that rose in my throat. I needed to concentrate on my sister right now; there would be plenty of time for anger when Stephen got home tomorrow. Though I was a little concerned about how that was going to go.

I already knew I was going to confront him the minute he walked in the door; that much I could not avoid doing. I was planning on sending the girls over to Dad's; it would be better that they not know anything was going on, let alone hear any of it. I had not decided if I should send Kaedyn over there, too, or let her stay with me. Undoubtedly, she would want to stay, terrifying as it might be for her. But what I needed to decide was which way would be best for her.

And then there was the matter of making sure I was not alone with Stephen – either with or without Kaedyn. Based on what Kaedyn had told me about his threats, I was more than a little afraid that he would hurt one or both of us. But how to accomplish that?

I had all but settled on letting Kurt in on what was going on and asking him to be there with me when Stephen got home. But I was wondering if I should also have a stronger presence there. Like the police. Probably a good idea, but how could I get a police officer to sit at my house with me "just in case" without filing some kind of report? Would they do that? I wasn't sure.

"No!" Kaedyn shouted suddenly, sitting up quickly and flailing her arms.

The sudden outburst startled me, but I quickly shifted

gears. "Shh, Kady, it's okay." I took her hot face in my cool hands and made her look at me until her eyes focused. She blinked several times, and her breathing slowed. Her forehead and hair were drenched with sweat. I was amazed that there had been no other signs of her nightmare until her shout.

"It's okay, Kady, you're safe."

She nodded, her breathing steady but ragged.

"What happened? In your nightmare?" I asked softly.

"He – he came here. He came in my bedroom. He showed me what he would do to you if – if – if I told you what he was doing." Tears began to stream silently down her face.

I pulled her close. "You're safe, Sweetie. He's not here."

"It hurt, Kallie," my sister whimpered. "It hurt me, and he told me he would make sure that when he did it to you, it would hurt even more."

"Shh," I smoothed Kaedyn's damp hair back from her face. "He's not going to hurt me, and he's not going to hurt you anymore either. I promise."

Kaedyn nodded, but the tears did not stop.

My mind was racing, trying to figure out what he could have done to her, but I knew it was information I might never learn.

After a few minutes and a few deep breaths, Kaedyn

calmed down again. "Kallie," she whispered.

"Yes, Honey?"

"Did Stephen ever – did he ever do anything to you... that – you know..."

I was puzzled. "That hurt me?" I guessed.

"Yeah," Kaedyn whispered.

"Well..." I thought back. "Not intentionally. Not that I can remember, anyway."

"Not intentionally?"

"Well Kady..." I hesitated. Should I be doing this?

Kaedyn frowned at me. "What's wrong?"

"It's just... We've never really talked about sex, even though we probably should have. Do you really want to talk about it now?"

My sister shrugged. "I guess I just... I want to know that... that it isn't really like... like that."

"Ohhh." That thought had never occurred to me. Now it made sense. "Well, Honey, it's just that sometimes... things hurt a little bit. Especially the first time you try them."

Kaedyn's face was blushing a brilliant shade of pink, but her features were still twisting up in that way that told me she was trying to work something out. I was watching her intently, and the moment she raised her eyes, I caught her gaze. "What is it?"

"I'm just wondering if... if the things he did... if they were – were..." she was searching for something. "Normal," she finally said.

I sighed. Nothing about this situation was simple. "Normal is relative, Sweetie. Nothing that he did to you was normal. Because it never should have happened. Between a loving, consenting couple, that might be different. But this... Sweetie, this was... sick and dysfunctional and manipulative and controlling. It was, in every possible way, wrong. So there is absolutely no way to apply the word 'normal' to this situation."

"Yeah."

"Come on, Sweetie. Let's see if we can get some rest, okay? It's quarter to four in the morning."

"Okay. I'll try."

"It's going to be okay, Kade." This time when she fell asleep, she slept for three and a half hours.

Kaedyn

When I woke again, it was because Kallie had shifted. The sun was shining through my windows, and I blinked in the bright light. My right arm was asleep, and when I sat up, pins and needles shot up and down my arm.

Kallie was already sitting up, sitting with her legs crossed, watching me. I scowled at her as I shook the tingling feeling out of my arm.

"Sorry," she said. "You were sleeping peacefully, and I was enjoying that. I have a feeling it's... been awhile."

I nodded resignedly and glanced at the clock. It was almost seven thirty. "Wow."

"Yeah. See what I mean?"

I looked around. "Did it... was it... was it a dream? Did everything that I remember... really happen last night?"

Kallie reached out and gently rubbed my arm. "It wasn't a dream."

I sighed.

"It's okay, Sweetie."

269

"I never... I was never going to tell you any of that."

"I'm glad you did," Kallie whispered.

A wave of panic washed over me. "Kallie, he – he's coming home today." I jumped up and started moving quickly around my room. I picked up dirty clothes off my floor, straightened the books on my desk, all the while muttering to myself, "He's going to find out, he's going to find out; what am I going to do, what am I going to do?"

Kallie stood up and calmly but firmly caught me by the wrists, holding me still. "It's going to be okay, Kady. You're going to be okay."

"He's going to know, Kallie. He's going to know."

"Yes, he is, Sweetie. Because I'm going to tell him. And he's not going to hurt you anymore. I promise."

I looked around wildly. My mind was racing. "What do you mean, you're going to tell him?"

"You and the girls are going to go to Dad's after breakfast. I'm going to ask Kurt to be here with me when Stephen gets home. And then I'm going to tell him that I know what he's done, and I'm going to ask him to leave."

I shook my head. "No, Kallie. No way."

"What?"

"I'm not going to Dad's, Kal. No way. I'm going to be with you."

270

"Kady," she said softly.

"No, Kallie. No."

"Fine. I guess I knew you wouldn't want to go. I had to try."

I nodded. "I'm staying here," I said, just to be clear.

"Okay."

"Mommy?" The tiny voice was out in the hall. Kallie quickly reached up to gently touch my cheek before turning to go to the door.

"In here, Baby," she said as she opened the door. Celia ran into her mother's arms.

"Aunt Kade!" she cried when she saw me.

"Morning, Ceely," I said, smiling at her. She grinned and flapped her hand at me in her adorable way of waving.

"Should we go downstairs and get some breakfast?" Kallie asked.

"Yeah!" Celia said enthusiastically. Kallie swung the four year old onto her hip and headed down the stairs.

"Would you mind getting Brooke up?" she asked me.

I nodded and went to the girls' room.

Brooke was already sitting up in her toddler bed, smiling happily at me. "Aunt Kay!" she exclaimed, holding her arms out wide.

I was across the room in just a few steps and scooped

271

her up, swinging her around in a big circle. She squealed with delight.

"Ready for breakfast?"

She nodded. I hugged her tightly, and we went downstairs to join our sisters for breakfast.

Kallie made waffles that morning. It reminded me of when she would come home from college when I was little and make me waffles for breakfast. Her waffles had always been my favorite. I was only able to eat a few bites before I began to feel sick, but I fought the need to run to the bathroom and throw up. I could feel Kallie's eyes on me when I put down my fork, but I figured if I was going to stay out of the bathroom, she could live with me not eating any more right now.

The girls, however, ate hungrily. I watched Kallie move around the kitchen nervously, cleaning things up, moving things around. I knew she was trying to keep herself busy. She caught my eye over the girls' heads several times, and she just held my gaze steadily for several minutes, giving me strength, silently reminding me that everything would be okay.

When Brooke and Celia had finished, Kallie put their plates in the dishwasher, washed their hands and faces, and followed them upstairs to get them dressed.

I sat at the kitchen table, looking around the room. The kitchen was spotless; Kallie must really be nervous.

A noise at the front door startled me, and I jumped several inches in my chair. Taking a deep breath, I moved quietly into the living room and carefully lifted a corner of the curtain to look out the window. Someone was standing on the front porch. But before my heart could start pounding, he stepped off the porch. It was only the mailman.

I shakily let out the breath I had been holding in.

Then I looked down and realized I was still wearing my pajamas. I glanced at the door to make sure it was still bolted shut from the night before, then headed upstairs.

I could hear Kallie and the girls moving around in Brooke and Celia's room just down the hall from mine. They were laughing and sounding like they were having fun. The laughter sounded foreign to my ears. I wondered if I would ever laugh again.

I rolled my eyes at my own cliché thoughts.

But would I?

Pulling myself from the dark thoughts, I began to dig through my drawers for something to wear. I finally settled on jeans and my favorite navy blue and tan sweater. When I got nervous, I tended to get cold. The sweater would both keep me warm and give me a feeling of security. I grabbed a short sleeved navy blue tee shirt to wear under the sweater.

I looked at the clock on my night stand. It was eight

273

thirty. I thought Kallie had said Stephen would be home around noon, but I could not remember for sure.

The thought of him had me in a panic again.

Grabbing the clothes I had picked out, along with underwear and socks, I listened for my sister and nieces; they were still in the girls' room, and it sounded like Celia and Brooke were getting hyper and bouncing around while Kallie tried to get them to get dressed. I reached into my clothes hamper and found my jeans from yesterday; I pulled the little tissue wrapped package from the pocket. Then I slipped out of my room and went to the bathroom.

In the bathroom, I dropped my clean clothes on the top of the toilet and got a clean towel out of the closet. I turned on the water as hot as I would be able to stand it and stripped off my pajamas. Then I took one blade from the little tissue wrap, and tucked the tiny packet away in the pocket of the clean jeans on top of the toilet.

The steam in the room was already hot and thick by the time I climbed into the shower, holding the blade carefully in my thumb and first finger. I let the hot water wash over me for a minute or two. I was freezing, but I didn't think the water would help much with that. Still, it felt good. It helped to wash away some of the feelings of grime all over my body, feelings of his hands on me; but the water could not wash away the feeling that he had left part of himself behind on me, like permanent fingerprints.

I lifted the hand holding the blade. I had been trying to hold back the cutting for awhile now, because of the way Stephen had used it. I had not been able to stop cutting completely – the need for the tangible pain was too great – but I had been careful to make small cuts and only in places Stephen would not readily notice. It had been so hard to hold back from allowing myself to feel the depth of physical pain I really needed to feel; but today I no longer had to deny myself that. Because Kallie had promised she would never let him touch me again. He would never see the marks. He would never be able to do any of those things he had done to me in the name of helping me. Now I could finally be free of the pain he had inflicted on me for so long. Now I could find comfort and healing in this real, physical pain, which took away all the other pain.

So I let go.

I let go of the control that had kept me making short, shallow scratches for the last two and a half months. I let go of caring about the permanent effect of my self-medicating. I let go of being careful.

I let go of keeping track of time.

I had no idea how much time had passed when I

realized Kallie was banging frantically on the door. "Kade? Kaedyn! What's going on? Are you okay?"

"Um..." I looked around. I must have been blocking everything out, the way I had learned to do in Stephen's office. "I'm okay, Kallie," I called. "Sorry!"

"Kady, open the door."

"Just a minute, Kal. I'm fine."

I could almost hear my sister's exasperated sigh.

As I glanced around the shower, I gasped softly in disbelief. The bath tub floor was a bright red, coated in splattered blood. I tried to keep my voice calm; I needed to convince her that I was okay, and remaining calm was imperative to accomplishing that.

"I just zoned out, Kallie. I'm fine. Just let me finish up my shower."

I must have sounded at least relatively calm, because after a moment of silence, during which my sister must have been weighing her options against my request, Kallie answered me. "Okay, but please try to hurry up."

"I will."

I waited until I heard my sister walking back down the hall before I panicked.

There was blood everywhere. Not only was the floor covered, but the shower curtain was spattered with it, and it was all over my hands and arms and legs. What had I done?

I searched my body frantically for the source of the blood, and finally found three sources: the front of my left shoulder and both of my thighs about six inches above my knees. I wasn't sure what to do first: try to staunch the flow of blood, or clean up the mess I had made. My common sense told me that I needed to stop the bleeding first, or I would just continue to bleed all over the place as I tried to clean up; but I felt a compulsion to clean up the blood before someone saw it. I forced myself to make it the priority to get my cuts cleaned up and taken care of first.

Careful to avoid the rug, I climbed gingerly out of the shower and found a couple of dark colored towels in the closet and climbed back into the shower. I took the removable hand held shower head off the holder and used it to carefully wash the excess blood off myself. Then I decided it would be easiest to clean up some of the blood in the shower while I was already in there, so I sprayed off the shower curtain and rinsed most of the blood that was on the floor down the drain, taking the time to rinse the bottoms of my feet. I had to make sure I did not leave anything behind that would alert my sister to what had just happened.

I realized with a start that the one and only person who knew about the cutting was Stephen.

The implications made me want to cut again. And then throw up. And then cut again.

I took a deep breath to steady myself. I needed to get this done so that I could convince my sister that I was okay. If she started to worry again, I was in danger of getting caught.

Once I had gotten as much cleaned up with the shower that I could, I climbed out of the shower, leaving the water on, and sat on the edge of the bath tub, wrapped in my towel. The cuts on the front of my shoulder were pretty deep, but they were not bleeding profusely, like the cuts on my legs were. So I used the extra dark blue towels to apply pressure to the cuts on my legs until the bleeding slowed. Then I found some gauze and bandaging tape in the medicine cabinet. It was a somewhat difficult task, but I eventually got the wounds securely bandaged. I also bandaged up the cuts on my shoulder, just to be safe. Then I dressed and used the dark blue towels to finish cleaning up the shower.

When I was satisfied that I had cleaned up every single drop of blood, I rinsed the excess blood out of the two dark towels and hung them on one of the towel racks to dry. Then I wrapped the used blade in a wad of toilet paper and buried it in the garbage, gathered up my things, and opened the bathroom door.

Kallie was standing there with her arms crossed.

Crap. I quickly thought back to make sure I hadn't made any incriminating sounds. I didn't think I had.

"What?" I asked, trying not to sound too defensive.

"Just wondering what was taking you so long."

I shrugged. "I told you, I needed to finish my shower. I tried to hurry, but I need clean hair."

"So what happened?"

"I just zoned out I guess. I'm sorry I scared you."

"I wasn't scared, just... concerned."

"Okay, well I'm sorry."

"It's okay. I was just getting the girls ready to go over to Dad's. Are you going to ride along with us?"

"Already? What time is it?"

"Just a little after ten."

"What?? I guess I really did zone out."

"Yeah."

"Yeah, I want to go with you. I think... I don't think I really want to stay here alone."

Kallie nodded. "Good. I don't think I want you to stay here alone either."

"Do I have time to dry my hair?"

"Yep."

I hurried to my room, dumped my dirty clothes in my hamper, and grabbed my hair dryer and a comb. In ten

279

minutes, my hair was mostly dry and pulled back into a pony tail. I hurried downstairs and found Kallie and the girls playing with a game on the living room floor.

"Ready when you are."

Kallie looked up. "Great. We're ready."

Brooke jumped up from the floor. "We're going to Grandpa's house!" she exclaimed excitedly.

"I know," I replied, grinning at her. "What are you going to do there?"

"Um... watch tee bee and pay outside!"

"Come on, Brooke," said Kallie. "Help Ceely pick up the game before we go to Grandpa's."

Still unable to contain her delight, she bounced around while helping her sister put the game away. Kallie stood up and got all three of their jackets out of the coat closet while the girls cleaned up. "I already texted Kurt and told him I needed some help with something," she said quietly. "He said he would be available."

"Yeah, but what is he going to say when he finds out what it is you want help with?"

"He'll be fine."

I raised an eyebrow at my sister's tone of complete certainty. "What aren't you telling me?"

"Well," Kallie cleared her throat. "Kurt wasn't exactly

any more thrilled about me marrying Stephen than you were."

"What??" This was the first I had heard anything to that effect.

"Yeah. He told me he didn't feel good about it. He admittedly didn't have anything to base it on, but asked me to rethink it. I was pissed. I told him I wasn't going to rethink anything based on his gut." The look on my sister's face was one of pure regret.

I could feel that my own eyes were wide with shock. I did not know what to make of the information, so I stored it away to deal with at another time.

"Ready, Mommy," Celia said, holding up the game box for Kallie to put away.

"Thanks, Baby. Let's go."

When we pulled into Dad's driveway, I started to shake uncontrollably. Kallie reached across the console and rubbed my arm. "It's going to be okay, Kady," she said softly. I just nodded. Then my dad came out of the house to help with the girls.

Kallie and I climbed out of the car and started to take the girls out of their car seats.

"Everything okay, Kallie?" My dad asked off to the side.

"Yeah, Dad, fine. Kaedyn and I are just going to take care of some things, and it will be easier without the girls under foot."

Kurt had followed Dad out of the house, and was standing on the porch with his arms crossed over his chest. He was watching me thoughtfully. I pretended not to notice.

"Bye, Mommy!" the girls said, giving Kallie hugs and kisses.

Dad took them in the house, with a "Call me if you need anything, Kal."

"Thanks, Dad." Then to Kurt, she said, "Why don't you follow us back?" He nodded without a word and got into his truck.

When we got home, it was ten forty-five. Kurt parked on the street in front of the house and followed us into the house.

In the kitchen, I sat at the table, watching my brother nervously. What was he going to say? What was he going to think?

"Do you want anything to drink?" Kallie asked. "I made iced tea."

"That would be great," Kurt replied. My sister looked at me, and I nodded. Kallie poured three glasses and sat down at the breakfast bar, which divided the kitchen in half and was up a little higher than the table.

Kurt took a drink. "All right, Kal. What's up?"

"Well, I need to begin by apologizing and telling you that you were right."

"What do you mean?"

"It has been made clear to me in the last few... hours... that I – I made a mistake when I married Stephen." Kallie drew a long breath, and it caught in her throat as she fought back tears. I immediately felt immense guilt at what I was putting my sister through.

"What do you mean?" Kurt repeated, looking from Kallie to me and back to Kallie again. "What's going on?"

"Kurt... Stephen has been... has been hurting Kade... for several months now."

"Hurting Kade? What do you mean, 'hurting Kade'? Wait... What?!?" My brother's anger, once he understood, was immediate and overwhelmingly intense.

"Kurt..." Kallie began, but Kurt cut her off.

"When does his plane get in?" he demanded. "I'll go straight there and meet him getting off. He won't get anywhere near this house again."

"Kurt, stop!" Kallie said firmly. "I am going to deal with this. You are not here so that *you* can deal with it. You're here to... well... basically so that Kade and I don't have to do it alone."

Kurt frowned. "Are you thinking he's going to get

violent?"

"Well..." Kallie looked at me, a question in her eyes. I nodded reluctantly. "He has... threatened... Kaedyn. He's threatened to hurt her further, and he's threatened her with hurting me. I just wanted to – to take every possible precaution."

"Why didn't you call the police?" The accusation in Kurt's voice pierced me.

"Because, Kurt, now is not the time."

"Now *is* the time, Kallie! What if he gets really violent? What if he goes crazy and kills all of us?"

"He won't."

"What you mean to say is that you want your chance to give him a piece of your mind."

"Well, there is that. But honestly, Kurt, I didn't think the police would come without me making some kind of formal report, and Kaedyn isn't ready to do that yet."

Kurt looked at me with surprise. "Why not?"

I didn't answer him right away, but I was looking at Kallie with the same surprise Kurt had just had on his face. "I – I'm just not, Kurt," I replied simply. Aside from the fact that I was shocked that Kallie was not going to fight with me over filing the report, I was not in any kind of frame of mind to fight with Kurt over it right now.

He looked back to my sister. "Kal, you have to make her file a report."

"No, I don't, Kurt. That's her decision to make, and hers alone. It isn't my decision and it certainly isn't your decision. Besides, that isn't the point. I just asked you to be here so that he would think twice about getting violent when I confront him."

Kurt inhaled deeply. Finally he nodded. "Okay. Then I have another proposal."

Kallie just looked at him expectantly.

"Nate."

Kallie was visibly startled by the mention of the name. "Nate? What about Nate?"

"He's a police officer, remember? If he's off duty today, maybe he would be willing to come over, you know, for reinforcement."

Kallie's eyebrows shot up. "Interesting idea."

Kurt nodded and pulled out his cell phone. After a moment, he said, "Nate. Kurt. Hi. Not too bad, how about you?" Pause. "That's good. Hey are you on right now?" Pause. "How would you feel about helping me out with something?" Pause. "Well, I'm at my sister's house. Yes, Kallie. Her husband is going to be home from a business trip soon, and she's about to give him some... upsetting news. I was wondering if you would mind coming over for a bit, you know, to sort of be a calming influence." Pause, longer this time. Then Kurt grinned. "You drive a hard bargain. For sure. Thanks, buddy. You remember how to get here?" Pause. "Yep, that's it. Thanks again. See you soon." Kurt hung up his phone. "He's on his way. I have to buy him lunch tomorrow for payment." Kurt chuckled to himself.

Kallie's eyes were wide, reflecting mine, I was sure. "Wow. Thanks, Kurt."

"No problem. So what time is he supposed to be home?"

"Noon," Kallie replied, glancing up at the clock on the wall. I looked too. It was just a few minutes after eleven o'clock. "His plane is probably coming in right about now."

I felt suddenly sick to my stomach. "I'll be right back," I said, getting up from the table and bolting from the kitchen.

Kallie followed me to the bathroom. This time, she did not try to dissuade me from throwing up; she just sat next to me on the floor and held my hair out of my face. I had no control over it anymore anyway; I did not need to do anything to force my body to purge itself, but I could not have done anything to prevent it, either. Kallie just sat quietly, holding up my hair with one hand, and rested the other cool hand on the back of my neck.

When I finished, I brushed my teeth to get rid of the taste. "You can stay in your room if you want," Kallie said gently.

I shook my head. "No. I'm going to be there." I could not tell my sister that the main reason I needed to be there was to make sure Stephen did not take the opportunity of my absence to try to convince my sister I had lied to her.

Kallie hugged me tightly.

"Are you scared?" I whispered against her shoulder.

"A little," she admitted. "But it's going to be okay, Kady. You'll see."

"Yeah." He had said that, too, every single time.

Kallie

By the time Stephen's BMW 5 Series pulled into the
drive next to my Camry, I was a bundle of nerves. With Kurt
and now Nate here, I was not really worried that anything
would go wrong procedurally, but I was still concerned about
how Stephen would react.

Even though I sometimes thrived on necessary
confrontation, I still hated it.

We had decided that the living room would be the best
place to wait. It was the first room just inside the front door,
and Stephen would not have a chance to get into other parts of
the house. Nate agreed with our reasoning. He had also liked
that it was open and uncluttered, just in case.

We had not given Nate any details on what the
confrontation was going to entail. I knew he would hear
everything anyway, and I figured it was just better that way.
Especially since a huge part of it was going to be about him. I
felt bad that he was about to get dragged into our fight without
even knowing it, but I knew that trying to explain it all to him

beforehand would take too long.

Nate had parked his car up the street a ways, so that Stephen would not know he was there prior to walking into the house. Now, Nate and Kurt sat on the couch, out of the way but facing the front door. Kaedyn was fluttering about nervously, twisting up her fingers and constantly rubbing the palms of her hands on the fronts of her jeans. I wanted to go to her, to take her in my arms and calm her, but I knew it would just make her more nervous; so I left her alone.

Stephen was coming up the front walk. He was opening the door. He stopped in his tracks when he saw me standing there and Kaedyn pacing the entry way to the kitchen.

"Hi, Babe," he said to me, looking slightly stunned when I did not move. "Is Kurt here?"

"Kurt's here," I said, motioning to the couch.

"Oh, hi Kurt. Thought that was your truck out there." Kurt nodded but did not get up from the couch. "And this is...?" Stephen nodded toward Nate.

"Surely you remember Nate," I said. "We used to hang out with him and his sister all the time."

Slight recognition dawned on his face. I couldn't tell if he really didn't remember, or if he was hiding it. "Oh yeah. Mel, right?"

Nate nodded solemnly. Stephen turned back to me.

Kaedyn was clenching and unclenching her hands at her sides.

"What's... going on, Kallie?" Was it my imagination, or did he look slightly nervous.

I hardened my gaze, to hide any fear that might be lingering in my eyes. "What's going on, Stephen, is that you're leaving."

"Excuse me?"

"I learned this week what a huge mistake I made when I married you, and I don't want you to be here anymore. So I am asking you to please leave. I'll be calling my lawyer later on today." I was amazed at how calm and matter of fact I was.

He did not look nearly as stunned as I had thought he should. He did, however, look every bit as angry as I had expected. I glanced at Kaedyn out of the corner of my eye. She had her right arm crossed over in front of her and was pressing against the front of her left shoulder so tightly that her knuckles were turning white.

Stephen was watching her closely. He took a deep breath and spoke again without taking his eyes off her. "Kallie. What is going on?"

"I think you already know. In fact, I can tell by the way you are intently watching Kaedyn that I am making the right decision."

His eyes jerked back to me. "So help me, Kallie; tell me

291

what is going on right *now*."

"Kaedyn has told me what you've done, what you've been doing." His eyes hardened with anger, but he remained otherwise perfectly still. "It's over, Stephen. You're not going to touch her ever again. You're finished. It's over."

He was completely silent and completely still, and for one very long minute, I thought all of our concerns had been for nothing and he was just going to be resigned and leave.

And then all the manipulating psychology crap that I had been expecting all along began to flow freely. "Is – is that what she told you? That *I* was the one who touched *her*? Kallie, you have to understand – " he cast a concerned look at Kaedyn - "she is very troubled. She's been very deeply troubled since your mom died."

I watched my sister closely. She was starting to panic; I could see it plainly in her eyes, even though she was trying desperately to keep it off her face. She was terrified that I was going to believe his lies.

"No, Stephen," I cut him off. "She's been deeply troubled ever since you started molesting her!" My voice quickly escalated into a shout. I had been needing to shout for many hours now, and with the girls out of the house and the object of my anger in front of me and an off-duty police officer with a gun behind me, I could finally let loose.

"Kallie, look." He looked at Kaedyn again. "I don't blame her." He took a step toward my sister. "Kady, I don't blame you. You're hurting. You need someone to take it out on. It's perfectly understandable."

But I erupted at his use of my nickname for her. "Don't you call her that! Don't you *dare* call her that! You are not going to take anything else away from her, do you hear me?! I won't let you!"

He took a step back again and threw his hands up in a gesture of surrender. "Kallie, honest," he said calmly. "I didn't touch her. I haven't done anything wrong, except maybe to try to help her with a problem that I probably should have sent her to a real therapist for. But don't you remember? You're the one who suggested I talk to her. And honest, Kallie, I wouldn't do that. I've only ever thought of her as a little sister."

His ability to remain calm was making me feel like I was looking like a crazy idiot to my brother and Nate.

Then Kaedyn spoke. "You're a liar," she said, almost in a whisper. "The things you did to me..." she shuddered and her grip on her shoulder tightened. I moved to her side and put my arm around her.

"Did you think I would never find out, Stephen?"

"I can't believe you're believing her over me," he replied. "Don't you understand what grief can do to a person?

293

She obviously needs more attention from you in order to deal with the loss of your mom, and she's made these accusations up in order to get you to pay attention to her. And look, it's worked, hasn't it?"

I made a little growling sound in my throat. "You're a liar. I know what you've done to her, Stephen, and it doesn't have anything to do with Mom or getting attention from me."

"Kallie," he reached for me. "I swear to you. I would never touch Kaedyn like that any more than I would Celia or Brooke."

That only served to set me off again. "And did you?!" I yelled at him. "Did you touch my little girls?!?"

"No!" he yelled back. "I just told you, I would never do that. What do you think I am, Kallie? Maybe you're the one who needs help!"

"I swear to God, Stephen!" I was ready to lunge at him and damn the consequences. "You're lucky Kurt and Nate are here right now. If they weren't, I'd rip some parts off of you that you would dearly miss!"

Stephen's eyes grew wide for just an instant, and then he recovered and just shook his head. "I think you and Kade both need to see a therapist. For psychotic delusions."

Nate stood up. "Stephen, I think it's time for you to leave now."

Stephen rounded on him, unable to contain his anger this time. "I don't know who you think you are, but I have no intention of going anywhere. This is my own home, and I'll leave when I'm damn well ready!"

Nate just lifted his chin and regarded Stephen silently. I wished I had a gun on my hip, so I could be that calm.

Stephen turned back to me. "What is he doing here, anyway, Kallie?"

"I'm surprised you don't remember him better, Stephen." I watched his face for a reaction. He remained carefully in control of his expressions. I knew he must remember Nate and what he had done to him, and to me. I had originally planned to throw the incident in Stephen's face and dare him to deny it, but now I decided to try a different tact. "Nate," I said, "do you remember the summer when Stephen and I got married?" Nate nodded. "Do you remember anything... weird... happening that summer?"

Nate thought for a moment, and then shook his head. "I don't recall anything?"

"I didn't think you would." I glanced sideways at Stephen, who continued to remain impassive. Then I looked over my shoulder at my sister, to make sure she was still doing okay; she had been eerily silent this whole time, and it scared me a little bit. "That's because Mel interrupted the little plan

that was laid," I continued, turning back to face Nate.
Stephen's eyes narrowed. "Oh not to worry," I said in a
sarcastically reassuring tone, "your plan still played out as you
hoped. It was just Mel who found the little... present you left.
Not Nate."

Nate looked puzzled. Stephen held my gaze steadily, as
if daring me to continue. "I, of course, was the one to find the
other little gifts you left in my drawer. The thing is, Stephen...
that stunt had nothing whatsoever to do with my accepting
your proposal. I can't help but wonder, though, if the belief
that you manipulated me into marrying you has affected you in
more ways than one over the past nine years."

Stephen's nostrils flared as he took in a breath through
his nose and tried not to explode with anger.

"Here's the thing, Stephen. I was not the first one to
discover what you did."

His jaw tightened. And then it hit me.

Kaedyn spoke before I could. "It was me. I was
playing in my bedroom, and I saw you digging around in her
drawers. I saw you put something in your pocket, and I saw
you leave something there, in the drawer." Across the room,
Kurt's jaw dropped. Wisely, he remained silent. "I just didn't
know for sure what it was. Then Kallie figured it out when
she... read it... in my..." Kaedyn had just figured it out too.

296

"You knew she knew." I was amazed at how calm I was now. I glared at my husband, unable to keep the hatred from my eyes. I was surprised – and disappointed – that angry red lasers did not shoot out of my eyes and disintegrate him on the spot.

"He read my journal," Kaedyn whispered. I moved back to her, putting my arm around her while also trying to keep my body as a shield between her and Stephen. She was trembling uncontrollably.

"So what was it, Stephen?" I demanded. "Some twisted form of punishment for seeing what you had done? Or a really sick way to drive a wedge between her and me so that I would never find out what you had done? Or maybe a little bit of both?!?"

He remained silent.

"I could rip your eyes out," I said viciously. My voice quickly raised to a scream. "Do you have any idea what you've done? She's a *child*, Stephen! A *child*! She was only a baby when it happened – she didn't even know what she was seeing!! How could you do this?!?"

"You're wrong," he said quietly when I had stopped to catch my ragged breath. "You have no idea what you're talking about. This is a very interesting story, but it simply is not true."

Kaedyn was crying softly behind me. Stephen looked at

297

her. "I don't know what would make you make up such incredible stories, but you know the truth. These things simply did not happen. I strongly suggest that you tell your sister right now that you've been lying to her."

Had he just threatened her right in front of me? I looked helplessly over at Nate and Kurt. Nate spoke up. "That sounded an awful lot like a threat, Stephen. I really do think it's time for you to leave now."

"You misunderstand me," Stephen said, in his best "I honestly meant no harm" voice. "I only meant that for her own mental health, she really should admit to her own lies and start to deal with her problems straightforwardly. It's the only way she'll ever get better."

Nate was unconvinced by his manipulative crap. "I know as well as you do, that's not what you meant. Now," he looked at me with a question, and I nodded, "it's time for you to leave."

Stephen stared coldly at Nate for a moment, and then turned back to me. "What are you going to do?"

"I told you, I'm calling my attorney."

"And then what?"

"And then I'm leaving you."

"You would leave me over a lie? Over a – an accusation that can't be corroborated?"

"I don't have any reason not to believe her, Stephen. Kaedyn has never lied to me. You have. And furthermore, she has never been an attention seeker. So your plan is flawed. You've tried to pin characteristics on her that just aren't realistic for her personality and past behaviors. You of all people should have known better. Kind of a sophomoric mistake, wouldn't you say?"

I was amazed at how confident I felt. Now Stephen was the one getting more and more angry by the minute. I expected to see steam start to pour from his ears any second now.

"All right," he said, looking from Kaedyn to Nate to me. "I'll go. But where are the girls? I want to talk to them."

"They're somewhere safe." Suddenly I started to panic that I had picked the wrong place to send them, that he would easily find them there. I should have sent them somewhere else, someplace he would never think to look for them.

"They're going with me."

It was hard to stifle an outright laugh. "Over my dead body."

"Don't tempt me," he muttered before he could stop himself.

"Let's go!" Nate said roughly, grabbing Stephen's arm.

"Let go of me!"

For a split second, I was afraid Stephen would hurt Nate, but Nate held his upper arm tightly. "No, sir. That was your second overt threat in the last ten minutes. We are leaving."

Stephen went out the door with Nate, but Nate never let go of his arm.

"I'll get the girls, Kallie!" he called back over his shoulder. "I'll get those girls and you'll never see them again!"

I shuddered. "I will never let that happen," I promised, more to reassure myself than anyone else.

And then Nate had dragged him out of earshot. I stood at the door and watched as Nate shoved Stephen into the back of his squad car and then got into the driver's seat. They sat there for several long minutes, but I could not drag myself away from the door. I wondered what Nate was doing. Then, finally, Nate got out and opened the back door. Stephen climbed meekly out of the back seat, and Nate walked him back down the street and to his own car. He stood in the driveway with his arms crossed until Stephen drove away; then he walked back to the house.

"He won't be back," Nate assured me.

"How can you be sure?"

"He won't be back." Nate would not say any more than that.

300

I was baffled. What had happened in that squad car?

I did not have time to worry about it, because when I turned to lead Nate back into the house, Kaedyn was not there.

"Where did she go?" I asked Kurt, trying hard to swallow my panic.

"To the bathroom, I think," he replied with a slight shrug.

"I'll be right back," I said quickly, and ran up the stairs taking them two at a time.

Sure enough, the bathroom door was closed. I tried the door knob; it was locked.

"Kade, open the door."

"Just a minute, Kal. Sheesh, I'm just using the bathroom."

Then why was my heart pounding so hard?

There wasn't a sound from inside the bathroom for several minutes. Then I heard the water running briefly. I paced back and forth in front of the door until she opened it. Then I pounced on her.

"What's going on?"

"I'm fine."

But she wouldn't look me in the eye. She brushed past me and headed for her bedroom; I followed.

She finally spoke. "What if he comes back?" Her voice

was trembling.

"Nate said he won't come back."

"How does Nate know?"

I shrugged, even though I was behind her and she couldn't see me. "I'm not really sure, but he was certain he wouldn't."

In her room, I thought Kaedyn was about to lie down on her bed, but then at the last minute, she switched directions and sat in her desk chair. I hated that he had taken from her the ability to lounge on her bed like an ordinary teenager.

"What are we going to do now?" she asked. Now she lifted her eyes to meet mine, and the helplessness on her face made my breath catch in my throat.

"We're going to call the locksmith and then the lawyer. Once the locksmith has come and changed the locks, we'll go get the girls. And then... then we'll move on."

"How?" Kaedyn whispered.

"We'll find a way, Kade. We're going to get through this. Together."

She nodded. "Kallie?"

"Yeah?"

"Can – can we move?"

"Absolutely." I had already begun trying to think about where we should go, and even started mentally packing the house. I had even gone so far as to consider starting to pack that night so that when we found a new house, we could move immediately.

She nodded again. Then she was silent.

"I need to go back downstairs and talk to Kurt and Nate for a few minutes. Will you be okay up here?"

She thought about that for a second. "I think I'll come with you. I don't really want to be in here by myself right now."

I was relieved. I had been somewhat worried about leaving her alone. Then I stopped, frozen by my own thought. Why had I been worried? What had had my heart pounding so violently as I had waited for her come out of the bathroom just a few minutes ago? I turned to ask her, but she was standing there beside her chair, ready to follow me from the room.

"You know what? Hang on just a second, okay? I'll be right back."

Kaedyn

I didn't know precisely what the look in my sister's eyes
meant, but I had a general idea, and I didn't like it. But I was
pretty much still stunned, which put me in an obedient mood,
so I sat back down in my chair and dazedly watched Kallie
practically rush from the room.

I thought back over the last couple of hours. They had
passed so quickly, and so much had happened. I was trying to
wrap my head around everything, but it was too difficult. I
didn't know what to think. I was overwhelmed with questions
from my own mind. Did Kallie really know what Stephen had
done to me? Was he really gone? Was he gone forever, or
would he try to come back to hurt me, or Kallie, or the girls?
Did Kurt understand what had happened? Did Nate? Was
Kallie planning to tell them?

And with that last thought, I panicked.

I jumped up from the chair, unable to sit still, and paced
around my room. I couldn't go down there. What was she
saying to Kurt and Nate?

I couldn't believe I had done this. I couldn't believe I had told my sister all that I had. And there were still so many things she didn't know. Suddenly, my heart was pounding crazily and I was struggling for air. My breaths came in short, shallow gasps.

I stopped pacing and put my hands on my thighs, pressing hard against my jeans. Waves of pain washed through my upper legs. I was breathing normally again; my heart rate began to slow down. And then I heard my sister coming back up the stairs.

Kallie

"Listen, guys, I want a few minutes to talk things over with you, but it's going to have to be later on. Right now I need – I need to be with Kaedyn."

Kurt and Nate both nodded, understanding reflected in their eyes.

"No problem, Kal," Nate said softly, coming to stand by me.

"I – I know I owe you both a little more of... of an explanation..."

"No, Kallie," Nate interrupted me, placing a hand on my shoulder. "It's all right. Go. Kade needs you."

I nodded. "Thanks. Hey, feel free to look around and find something to eat." Then I turned and went back upstairs.

"Kady?" I said softly, slipping through her partially open door. She was standing halfway between her desk and her bed, half bent over, hands clasped over her knees. "Sweetie, are you okay?" I rushed to her.

Kaedyn slowly stood up. "Yeah, I'm – I'm okay."

"Come on, Honey, let's sit down." I tugged her hand gently, pulling her down to sit on the floor with me. "We need to talk." I watched my sister closely. Her face remained impassive as she nodded slowly. "For some reason, I... I get the feeling there's something you aren't telling me." She just sat there, her eyes locked with mine, her expression unchanging. I waited a minute, and when she did not respond, I took a deep breath. "Care to share?"

Finally, after another long silence, Kaedyn spoke. "I don't know what you're talking about."

The phrase of the hour.

"Funny, I've heard that before. And it wasn't all that long ago."

"Well this time it's true. I really don't know what you're talking about."

I knew she was lying. Something in my core told me so. "What were you doing in the bathroom just a few minutes ago?"

"I was *peeing*, Kallie. Jeez."

Had I been overreacting? No, I argued with myself, I couldn't have imagined the sudden panic that had threatened to overwhelm me as I had waited for her to come out of the bathroom. "Kady..." I was having an odd sense of déjà vu as I realized I was about to beseech my sister once more to share her secrets. "Kady, you don't have to – to keep secrets anymore." I moved closer to her and reached for her. She didn't pull away this time. I put my arm around her shoulders and held her close to me. "We're done with that now. It's over. You can tell me anything. Certainly after... after what we've been through – what we're *going* through – you know that there's nothing you can't tell me." I took her face gently in my hands. "Please, Kade," I whispered, "I don't want to see you like this, hurting, hiding, feeling that you have to keep everything inside."

Kaedyn's expression softened. "I just – I don't know, Kallie. I mean – I mean, it's really not that big of a deal. I'm just... just thinking about things a lot."

I sighed. I knew that part was a lie too; whatever it was, it *was* a big deal. What could I say to get her to talk to me?

Kaedyn

You don't know what you're asking for! I wanted to scream at my sister. She had become too much of a mom, too much of a big sister to just be a sister, a friend. She would never understand my medicine; she would only see it through eyes colored with worry.

"Certainly after what we've been through – what we're *going* through – you know there's nothing you can't tell me." Her voice was so full of enticing compassion and tenderness, it made a little sister want to give in and spill everything.

But I feared this secret would be far more difficult for Kallie to swallow than the other secret had been.

"It's not that big of a deal, Kallie. I'm just... thinking about... a lot of things." I could not get past my fear that my sister would freak out, and then proceed to take away my medicine. I could not lose this; it was all I had right now.

"I'm sorry, Kade, but I just don't think you're telling me the truth. I've known you literally forever. I know you. I can tell when you're lying to me, and you're lying to me right now."

My face was in her hands, and I didn't have the energy to try to pull away from her, but I dropped my gaze from hers. I couldn't look her in the eyes; I was afraid I wouldn't be able to stop myself from telling her my secret.

"Now I know I'm right," Kallie whispered. She dropped her hands and turned to pace toward the door, then back toward me again. She walked back and forth several times, her arms wrapped tightly around her waist. She was at the door when she finally stopped, turned, and looked at me again. "What were you doing in there?" she asked in a soft almost-whisper.

I watched her, but I couldn't raise my eyes to meet hers. I knew my avoidance would just reinforce her notion that I was lying to her, but I couldn't force myself to make eye contact with her. If I did, she would not only see that I was hiding something from her, but she would see what exactly it was that I was hiding from her. I was walking a hairline fracture, desperate to keep my medicine a secret, and terrified that someone would somehow look at me and know I used it. The chances of that person being Kallie were astronomical.

"Kady," my sister held her arms out, palms up, in a gesture of helplessness, "tell me what to say; tell me what to do. Tell me how to help you." Kallie's voice was pleading.

"I – I want to tell you, Kal. But... I can't." *I don't*

know how. I don't know what to say. I don't know how
you will deal with it.

Kallie just shook her head slowly, disbelief passing over her features. "Kade. I honestly don't know what to do. I feel like you know you need to tell me... whatever it is. But I don't know what I can say or do to help you tell me."

Then an idea popped into my head. "Kallie, I – I *do* want to tell you. I just... I just need a little time. To – to think things through."

Kallie regarded me for several minutes that seemed like an hour, pondering my request. "All right," she finally said. "I can understand that." She seemed to be considering something more. "When can we... talk about it again? I mean, how much time do you need?"

I bit my lip. I had intended to buy myself some time to begin to appear normal again, as if nothing was going on, so that Kallie would forget about it and the whole thing would just drop. I hadn't planned on Kallie setting a time-based ultimatum. Panic threatened to overwhelm me yet again. "I – I don't really know, Kal. Can I... can I have a couple of days at least?"

"Whatever you need, Sweetie. I just... want you to know I'm here, and I'm willing to do whatever you need me to in order to help you get through... this."

I nodded. "Thanks, Kallie," I whispered.

My sister folded me into her arms. "It's going to be all right, Honey," she promised. I put my arms around her waist and held onto her tightly. I was afraid that if she let go, I would float away, out of her grasp, the only hold that was keeping me here anymore.

Kallie left my room that afternoon with a quiet resigned sigh, and after locking the door — out of complete habit — I sank fluidly to the floor and hugged my knees to my chest. I figured she had gone downstairs to talk to Nate and Kurt. I wondered how much she would tell them, but I was so drained that it was easier just not to think about it.

So naturally, I thought about other things instead.

Arms still wrapped around my knees, I shrank myself up into the smallest ball I could, and pressed my face against my knees. Pictures of Stephen hurting me began to flash before my eyes, like quick little snapshots taken with a camera. I squeezed my eyes shut more tightly, but it didn't make a difference; I couldn't keep the images out of my head.

I knew that somehow, in some way, it was my own fault he had hurt me. I should have stayed away from his office. I should have asked to go back to live with Dad. I should have told Kallie what he was doing to me. I should have followed

314

through with one of my many plans of joining Mom.

It suddenly hit me that all of the pain I had been dealing with, all of the hardship that was raining down on my sister, it was all my fault.

I felt a great weight beginning to press down on my chest. It grew heavier and heavier by the minute. I couldn't breathe. All I could think about was how I was putting my sister through hell because I hadn't been strong enough to stop Stephen from hurting me.

I was in a blind panic, moving as if in a dream, as I uncurled my legs and tugged my jeans down to my knees, slipping my tissue-wrapped razor blade from the back right pocket.

I had eighteen or twenty cuts on both legs. Some were long and fairly shallow; others were a little shorter but quite a bit deeper. They were all some varying shade of red; some pale pink scars, others scabbed over and beginning to heal, and still others angry and screaming and looking as if they might start to bleed again any second.

I gripped the blade tightly in my thumb and forefinger and pressed it to a place on my left leg where there were no scars. I was so overwhelmed with guilt and fear and self-loathing that for the first time, I did not have a plan before I started. I just knew I needed to do as much damage as possible.

There was a knock that sounded as if it was coming from the far end of a long tunnel. When my eyes came back into focus, I blinked against the light as if I had been shut up in a pitch black room for several hours. I was unsure how much time had passed, but as I looked down, I realized I didn't have time to worry about that.

Blood was pouring down both sides of both of my legs and onto the carpet. It was dripping from all of my fingers and the razor blade that I was still holding tightly. I was stunned and disoriented and... confused.

And then the knock came again, and I realized it was coming from my own bedroom door. *What do I do?*

"Kady? Kady, are you okay? Can I come in?"

"Um..." *What do I do?!?* "Just a minute!"

"Kady, you sound... Is everything okay?"

"I'm fine. I'm just – " I glanced around. "I'm just changing clothes. Just a minute." It was lame, and I knew it. But I didn't know what else to say. I also didn't know how I was going to fix this in only a minute. I jumped up and yanked my jeans up, forcing back the scream that threatened to escape my lips. I wiped my hands quickly on the back of my jeans, then tossed the razor blade in my desk drawer while grabbing an old throw blanket from the end of my bed. I tossed it over the blood on the carpet.

"Kaedyn!" Kallie was getting impatient.

I went to unlock the door. "I'm done. I'm sorry. Come in. I'm sorry." The words were coming out too fast, but I didn't know how to slow myself down. My heart felt like it was going to pound right through my chest.

Kallie wasted no time in bursting unceremoniously through my door. "Kady, are you okay? I've been knocking on the door for like two minutes. What's going on?"

"Nothing," I said innocently. "I was just sitting here thinking, and I must have dozed off. I've been kind of tired lately."

She nodded in understanding. "Maybe you should lie down and rest for a little while."

I nodded, having no intention of lying down but needing desperately to get her out of my room.

"Well anyway, Nate and Kurt are gone now. Nate gave me his cell number and told me to call if we need anything."

"That was nice of him." My own voice sounded far away.

"Yes, he – " Kallie stopped abruptly as a look of horror crossed her face. "Kady, what – what is on your jeans?" She moved swiftly toward me, her hand outstretched.

317

"Nothing," I said automatically, backing away from her.

"Kady, that's not nothing." Kallie's voice grew more alarmed with each word. "What is that? Is it – Kady, is that blood?"

I didn't know what to say. I was stumped for any more explanations or diversions, but I knew I couldn't let her see my legs. "No, I just – I must have just – spilled something," I stammered.

"Kady," my sister was bending over now, looking at my jeans. I tried to back away from her, but there wasn't really anywhere else to go; I was backed up to my desk chair. "That's blood!" Kallie shrieked. "Take those jeans off!" But she didn't wait for me to take them off; she reached out and unzipped them herself, pulling them down.

I yelped in pain, unable to hold it in.

"Oh... My... " Kallie didn't finish. For what seemed like several minutes, she was completely frozen, her eyes wide and her mouth in a small perfect 'o.' "Kady," she whispered, "what happened to you?" She stood slowly as her frightened eyes slowly met mine. Then she gasped. "Oh my gosh, we need to get you to a hospital."

"No, Kallie," I said. The firmness in my voice surprised me. "I don't need to go to the hospital. I just need to go in the bathroom and clean up. Honest. It will be fine."

She hesitated, then nodded, shock still fresh in her eyes. "Let's go. But if I can't get the bleeding to stop, you're going to the hospital." I stepped out of my jeans, and she gently led me from the room.

For the next hour, I spent each minute expecting my sister to start freaking out, waiting for an eruption that never came.

Kallie

It is hard to describe the feelings that flooded over me when I saw my little sister's bare legs. There were so many gashes that I couldn't even guess at the number of them, and they were bleeding profusely, having completely soaked the fronts of her jeans. I was shocked, and appalled... and I was scared. Who had done this to her? Had Stephen? Was this how he had kept her silent all this time? Something wasn't quite right about that explanation, but I was too worried about Kaedyn to think about anything else.

I had to get her to a hospital before she bled to death.

She protested. She could clean up in the bathroom, she said. I was in a state of utter shock, and I agreed. It seemed reasonable enough to at least clean her up and see how bad the cuts were before deciding on the hospital. Although I didn't plan to give her much time; if the bleeding didn't slow, she would pass out soon.

I helped her to the bathroom, where I sat her down on the top of the toilet and began pulling everything I could find from the medicine cabinet. I found a bag of cotton balls, two bottles of peroxide, antibiotic ointment, bandaids, squares of gauze, and medical tape. I dumped it all on the bath mat and knelt down in front of my sister.

Peroxide was the place to start. I looked at the cotton balls, then at my sister's legs. I shook my head at myself; cotton balls weren't going to do any good right now. I tossed them aside and picked up one of the bottles of peroxide. Quickly twisting off the lid, I poured it in a slow but steady stream over one of Kaedyn's legs and then the other. It ran onto the floor, but I didn't care. The first bottle was nearly empty when I thought most of the excess blood had been washed away. I soaked a wash cloth in warm water and gently cleaned away the rest of the blood that had begun to dry on her legs. As the blood was cleaned up, I was able to get a better look at the severity of the cuts. I gasped. There were so many, and they looked so awful and painful. I glanced up at my sister's face to see how she was holding up.

Her jaw was clenched tightly, and she was paler than I could ever remember having seen her before. I reached up and brushed her cheek with one crooked finger. "It's going to be okay, Kady," I whispered. She just nodded mutely. I wasn't sure what to make of it, but I pushed all that to the back of my mind. We would talk after I had her cleaned up and bandaged.

322

As I finished cleaning the cuts with the peroxide, I realized that not all of them were bleeding; there were several that were covered in new-looking scabs. However, as I bandaged the fresh cuts, I realized something. Stephen couldn't have done this; he'd been gone for days, and these were frighteningly new. So new that I was afraid to even think about how recent they actually had to be.

"Kady," I whispered. "When did this... happen?"

For the first time since I had burst into her room, Kaedyn met my eyes, but it was with an expressionless stare that I couldn't define. I could almost see the wheels in her brain spinning behind her deep blue eyes. She was trying to decide how to answer.

"Kade... just. Just tell me." My voice was still barely above a whisper.

Her eyes filled with tears, but they didn't spill over. I was forced to admit to myself that there was only one truth that made sense, no matter how opposed I was to believing it.

I was gingerly holding the bandage for the remaining cut. I looked closely at the cut; it was about two inches long, and such a deep red that I was sure it went deeper than I wanted to know. It was perfectly straight with perfectly smooth edges. I gently ran my thumb on the tender skin along the length of the gash. Then I carefully placed the bandage over the cut. With my fingers still resting gingerly on the one bandaged leg, I looked up at her again.

"You... You did this." I intended it to be a question, but it came out as a statement. It wasn't accusatory, but simply a statement.

Kaedyn swallowed hard. "I'm sorry, Kallie. I'm sorry." I could barely hear her; I had to read her lips to understand what she was saying.

I rose up to crouch on the balls of my feet and gently grasped my sister's arms just above the elbows. "Kade... Kady, what are you apologizing for?"

She sucked in a deep breath. "I didn't want you to – to – to – " She burst suddenly into tears. It seemed like she was trying to speak through her tears, but all I could make out were the uncontrollable sobs that were wracking her body. I swiftly rose to my feet and held my little sister close to me while she cried.

When her tears finally slowed, and she was breathing normally again, I spoke.

"Do you want to talk about it?"

She shrugged against my embrace. "What is there to say?"

"How about answering some questions?"

She shrugged again. When she didn't say anything, I

decided there wasn't any harm in at least trying. "How did you do this?"

She leaned back, and the look in her eyes was almost one of guilt. "I – I don't know if you really want to know that."

I swallowed hard. I couldn't help my sister if I was going to be queasy or unable to listen to what she had to tell me. I would listen calmly to anything she said; I wouldn't be judgmental or unreasonable, and I wouldn't "flip out," a term Kaedyn was fond of using.

"I do want to know. Please tell me how you did this."

"I – I used…" Her voice trailed off and she chewed on her lip for a moment. "I used a blade from my sh-shaving razor," she whispered.

I nodded, using every ounce of energy in me to keep my face unemotional. "Where is it now?"

"I threw it away," she replied, almost too quickly.

I frowned, but decided not to question her on it right now. I had taken some basic psychology classes for my teaching degree and license. From the small amount of literature I had read on the subject, taking away the instrument wouldn't stop her if she was determined to do it again. I needed to deal with the root of the problem, the motivation; and I needed to focus on finding the solution.

"How many times have you done this?"

Kaedyn shrugged. "I don't know. A lot."

"Every time he hurt you?"

"Pretty much."

"More than that?"

"Yeah."

I waited for her to expound on that, but she didn't. She wasn't going to volunteer any information that I didn't explicitly ask for.

"What other times… have you done it?"

She sighed. "When I thought about what he told me he would do if I told. When I… remembered him doing… things… to me. When I…" her voice grew so soft I had to strain to hear her. "When I pictured him… doing things… to you."

I felt my eyes widen slightly, though I fought the horror that threatened to cross my face. "What things, Sweetie?"

She shook her head, unwilling to tell me. "Just things."

"Things he said he would do? Or…?" I left a verbal blank, hoping she would fill it in.

She just shook her head again. "Just… sometimes things he – he said he would do. Sometimes just… sometimes things that he did to me and… and I wondered if he…" Her voice choked up just before she cut off. I could feel her anxiety

326

level rising, and I needed to shift directions before the anxiety progressed into full-blown panic.

"When did it start?" I asked quietly.

She paused a moment before answering. "I can't tell you that."

"What? Why?"

"I... I just can't."

"You mean you *won't* tell me."

"No..." Kaedyn shook her head in frustration. "I mean I can't. I don't... I don't really remember."

I felt my eyebrows scrunch forward in a frown. "How... is that possible?"

Kaedyn just shook her head. "I don't know, Kallie. I don't. I just... I don't remember."

Kaedyn

I was more frustrated with myself than with my sister. How could I not remember the first time I discovered the medicine? Actually, that statement wasn't entirely accurate. I remembered *doing* it very clearly; I just didn't remember *when* it happened. So I had no idea when it started or how long I had been using it. It felt like forever.

"Honest, Kal," I whispered, not wanting to hear the words out loud. "I don't remember when it was. I remember it, but..." Was it before Mom died, or after? It had to be after. Before I lost her, I'd never felt any pain like the pain that caused me to discover the medicine. Was I still living at Dad's, or had I moved in with Kallie? I wasn't sure. I locked eyes with my sister and slowly shook my head.

Kallie

My head was spinning with the complications. There was too much here for me to handle alone. And if I tried, all I would succeed at was in doing my baby sister a great injustice.

I needed to find help, and soon.

"We should pick the girls up and get some supper," I said softly.

Kaedyn nodded. "What about the locks?"

My eyes widened in surprise. "The locksmith has come and gone. He made quite a racket; you didn't hear him?" She shook her head. I sighed. "All the locks have been changed. There are two keys, and I have them both." Kaedyn nodded. I watched her for a moment, trying to gauge her emotional level. "I have a meeting with my attorney tomorrow. I asked Kurt to come over while I'm gone, but he has to work."

"That's okay; we'll be fine."

"Well, Kade, I didn't want to leave you and the girls here alone." I watched her very closely as I continued. "Nate volunteered to come stay; he's off duty again tomorrow."

There was only the slightest flicker of emotion across her face, and then her features were carefully impassive again. "Okay."

I frowned. "Is it really okay, or would it bother you?" I hated that she had become so impossible to read.

She swallowed hard. "I'll be okay." I couldn't tell if the stoic expression on her face was genuine or forced.

"Maybe you and the girls could come with me and just sit in the outer office," I mused aloud.

Kaedyn shook her head. "It will be fine, Kallie. Let's go get the girls."

I regarded her for a moment before nodding. "Okay, let's go."

Kaedyn was silent the entire time we were in the car. At Dad's, she waited while I went in to get the girls. She smiled at the girls when they greeted her enthusiastically, and then returned to staring blankly out her window. She completely ignored me when I asked what she wanted for dinner. The girls begged for McDonald's, and since they had been such great sports on such a stressful day, I gave in without thinking twice.

Celia and Brooke ate their chicken nuggets on the twenty-minute drive home, and as soon as we pulled into the driveway, I hustled them inside for baths and bedtime.

When I returned downstairs forty-five minutes later, I

found Kaedyn sitting in the overstuffed chair in the library, hugging her knees to her chest, staring off into space. I stood outside the doorway, debating whether or not to invade her space. Then, she looked up suddenly, and the vacant look left her face and was replaced with an attempted half smile.

"Hey, Kal. Sorry I wasn't much help with the girls."

I moved into the doorway and leaned against the doorjamb. "It's no problem, Sweetie. They're not your responsibility."

She just looked at me for a minute, her expression unreadable. "I guess I just don't want to be a burden to you," she finally said.

I went the rest of the way into the room and sat on the ottoman near the chair. "You're not, Honey," I said earnestly, reaching out to rub the back of her hand with my knuckle. "I need you to be here as much as you need to be here. I think maybe… I think maybe you're just feeling a lot of weight on your shoulders right now." She shrugged. "Listen, Sweetie," I ventured, "I want you to think about talking to someone."

Kaedyn cringed; she seemed to almost collapse in on herself. My heart broke a little bit, and I swallowed hard to force back the tears that I could feel beginning to rise up in my throat. "I know, Sweetie; I know you don't want to. But don't you see? It's the only way to work through all of this. It's the only way to heal from all the damage that's been done. You need to understand that none of this is your fault, and I – I'm worried you won't – I just don't think that's going to happen without really intensive... therapy."

I felt horrible and a little guilty bringing it up; after all, I had been so sure that talking to Stephen was the right thing to do and would help her. I had known it would be a very painful subject for her, and the last thing I wanted to do was cause my sister even more pain right now. But I was very afraid that if she didn't get help soon, she would spiral downward so quickly that I'd never be able to save her. So I was willing to allow a little more short term pain in order to ultimately help her.

Kaedyn was biting down hard on her lower lip. "I just – I just don't think I can do it, Kal."

I nodded. "I know you don't. But you will. It will take some time, but eventually, you will."

She shook her head stubbornly. "I'll never be able to trust anyone. Sitting in an office with a – therapist – will just make everything worse."

"Well then, we'll work something out so you're not *in* an office," I replied, just as determined as she was. "We'll figure it out. But you're going to see someone." Maybe it was too early for me to start being insistent, but I couldn't help it. Panic and fear for my sister's future were beginning to take over.

She didn't seem worried by my finality. "Forget it." She stood up and started for the doorway.

"Kaedyn Elisabeth."

She knew I meant business; I never used her full name. She stopped and turned, and the look on her face was the closest to anger that I had seen since Mom had died.

"What," she said stiffly.

I hated myself for the card I was about to play, but I was desperate. "You're going to see someone. It can either be with my help, or with Dad's."

"You. Wouldn't. Dare." Her words came out like stones, coarse and heavy.

I stared her down and waited for her to fold. She crossed her arms over her chest, and I knew she was trying to come up with some way around my ultimatum. I could tell when she couldn't find a loophole, because her eyes filled with tears.

She opened her mouth as if to say something, then stopped, closed her mouth, and very deliberately turned away from me.

I heard her feet pound on the stairs, and then her door slammed shut.

Kaedyn

I knew slamming my bedroom door was juvenile, but I didn't care. How could my sister do this to me?

Safely behind my bedroom door, I paced nervously all over the room, my mind racing furiously.

Would she really tell my dad? It was hard for me to imagine her doing that; but it was also nearly impossible for me to believe that my sister would not follow through, because she had never been given to empty threats.

I could not afford to take the chance that she would tell him. My life would be over; my dad would completely flip out. He would probably have me admitted to a hospital – possibly a psychiatric hospital – and I knew I would never survive in a place like that.

Come to think of it, I was kind of surprised *Kallie* hadn't flipped out. She had remained amazingly calm through the whole thing.

A thought hit me, and I stopped pacing in my tracks. Even when I had told Kallie about what Stephen had done, I had withheld the cutting from her. I hadn't trusted her to be able to deal with it.

But my sister knew everything now; she had seen my cuts and she knew I had done it to myself. She had remained calm while she had cleaned them up and asked me about how I had done it. Kallie had proven to me today that I could trust her beyond what I had thought I could. Maybe I should have confided in her sooner. Maybe I should have realized that I could trust her.

Maybe it wasn't too late to realize that. Maybe I should trust her now.

Kallie

I was still sitting in the library, trying to figure out how to fix the mess that had fallen into my lap, when my sister came back downstairs. She moved so quietly down the stairs and through the hall that I didn't even realize she was there until she was standing in the library doorway. She stood silently leaning against the door frame, thin arms crossed over her chest, for several long minutes. When she finally spoke, her voice was barely above a whisper.

"Okay, Kallie. I'll do it."

I inhaled deeply and just watched my sister, waiting to see if she would say more.

"But I – I want you to know…"

"What is it, Honey?"

Kaedyn shrugged slightly and fidgeted with the zipper of her hoodie. I reached over and patted the soft leather of the couch right beside me. "Come sit down, Sweetie. Let's talk about it."

She sighed, but came and sat down next to me. I

slipped my arm around her shoulders, and she leaned into me. "I'm scared, Kal," she finally whispered.

"I know, Sweetie." I wanted to tell her it would be okay. I wanted to tell her that whoever we found for her to meet with would be kind and trustworthy and not Stephen. I wanted to tell her I would never leave her alone with anyone ever again. But I didn't want to overwhelm her, so I just said, "I know."

We sat together in silence for several minutes before I felt hot tears running down my arm. I sat up and held my sister away from me just enough to confirm that she was crying; rivers of tears were streaming silently down her face. "Oh, Sweetheart." I sighed, wishing I could just take away my sister's pain. "What is it?"

"What if — what if she kn-knows?" Kaedyn hiccupped.

"Knows what, Honey?"

"Knows that — that it was my — " Kaedyn's sobs overtook her, and she crumpled into my lap. She shook uncontrollably as I held her and stroked her hair.

Then I realized what it was she had been about to say.

"Kaedyn," I said firmly. "You will hear this hundreds of times in the next few months, and maybe even years. But I'm going to say it now anyway. It was not. Your. Fault."

My sister continued to tremble, and shook her head in protest. But she didn't say anymore; just let me hold her until her tears subsided.

All I could think about was what a long road we had ahead of us.

Kaedyn

It *was* a long road. Or maybe I should say, it *is* a long road. Because it's a road I'm still on, a road I'll be on until the day I die.

Kallie called her attorney the next day, but not before she had tracked down a psychology major friend of hers from college. She had called her for a referral in our area, but it turned out Alex actually had her own practice nearby and offered to see me for a consult. Kallie spent several days telling me to think about it and decide if I was comfortable talking to someone she already knew. I knew my sister was feeling guilty about what had happened, and in the end, I decided that despite the fact that it was my brother-in-law that had hurt me, I still might be more comfortable with Alex than with a stranger, and decided to at least give it a try. Alex didn't even mind coming to the house to talk. Of course, that's all a different story, maybe for a different day, and maybe not.

Kallie also made me go to our doctor. I agreed to go for a general check-up and blood tests, but told her that I absolutely would not be taking my clothes off. I knew Kallie wanted to fight me on it, but she must have figured that convincing me to see Alex was a pretty big milestone for one day and she'd better not press her luck.

We found a new house pretty quickly, and I think Kallie may have been even more relieved about that than I was. I totally understand that too. I mean, she had lived in that house with Stephen for eight years. I would have been desperate to get away from eight years' worth of lies, too.

Sometimes people ask me if I've moved on. I kind of think that's a dumb question. I mean, of course I've moved on. I started moving on the night I told Kallie the truth about Stephen, and I've been moving on ever since. To me, the more important question is whether I'm the same person I was a year ago.

And of course, none of us is the same person we were a year ago.

But I also know I am not the same person I would have been if this past year had never happened.

If you or someone you know has been a victim of sexual assault, please get help.
Visit www.RAINN.org or call the
National Sexual Assault Hotline
1-800-656-HOPE (4673)

IF YOU ARE IN IMMEDIATE DANGER, CALL 911.

About the Author

Leigh has had a passion for children and teens since she was a young girl, and has been writing stories since she was six years old. Combining these two loves came naturally as a teen when she began writing short stories and poetry for teens. Leigh has a Bachelor of Arts in English from the University of Wisconsin, and has had several poems published in anthologies.

Lies That Bind: Kaedyn's Story is Leigh's first literary publication. Leigh lives in Wisconsin with her husband and five adopted children, whom she loves spending time with and learning from on a daily basis. When she isn't writing, she enjoys playing the piano and occasionally composes simple arrangements and accompaniments. She loves to read, almost as much as she loves to write. She enjoys cooking and baking and is also an amateur runner.

Leigh is currently working on two Young Adult novels for publication.

Other works by K. Leigh Michaels:

Lies That Bind: Lily's Story (Young Adult Fiction) **COMING SOON!**
Lies That Bind: Emma's Story (New Adult Fiction)
To Have a Family (Juvenile Fiction)
Contemplations (Poetry compilation, with Kevin Bissett II)

Learn more about K. Leigh Michaels and her upcoming works at her website: www.authorleighmichaels.com